A Love Unexpected

Under Kansas Skies Book One

Leah Brunner

Leah Brunner
AUTHOR OF SWEET ROMANCE

Leah Brunner Publishing

Contents

Dedication   I

Madden   II

1. Odette   1

2. Madden   8

3. Odette   19

4. Madden   24

5. Odette   32

6. Odette   43

7. Madden   52

8. Odette   59

9. Madden   66

10. Odette   77

11. Madden   83

12. Madden   89

13. Madden   94

14. Madden   100

15. Odette   107

16. Odette   117

17. Odette   121

18. Madden   127

19. Odette   132

20. Odette   140

21. Madden   150

22. Madden   156

23. Madden   161

24. Madden   170

25. Madden   175

26. Odette   183

27. Odette   186

28. Odette   194

29. Madden   197

Odette   201

     206

207

Acknowledgments   208

About The Author   209

To my husband, thank you for being my biggest cheerleader during this new adventure, and for never complaining when I spent countless hours hidden away in my writing cave. You are my hero and you will always blow away any book-boyfriend I could ever create.

Your love inspires me.

Madden

♥

Three Months Prior

Looking outside my parents' dining room window, I hear birds chirping as a light breeze blows petals off of my Mom's Bradford Pear tree. The serene scene is a stark contrast from where I'm standing. My eyes move from the window and back to the dining room where my entire campaign team is meeting for the first time.

Since my apartment isn't big enough to host this many people, my parents let us use their house for the meeting. They own a large home in the College Hill area of Wichita, Kansas. Their dining room is large and open, with bay windows and a massive table. The walls are painted a deep red, which looks very regal alongside the cherry wood table and matching chairs. And the fireplace makes the room feel cozy and inviting.

It's exhilarating to finally have everyone together in the same room. Looking around, I see papers scattered all over the table as everyone talks at once, sharing ideas and making notes. My cheeks are beginning to hurt because I can't stop grinning.

My team is made up of amazing people. There's my campaign manager, Paul Newhouse, whom I was fortunate enough to meet during my volunteer work. He's tall and slim with steel-grey hair and deep, brown eyes. He looks like he's all business. And he is. There's also my brother, David, who's a certified public accountant, who agreed to be my secretary. Along with Paul and my brother, there are a dozen others at our meeting: campaign strategists, graphic designers, and my public relations team. It's chaotic, but I can feel my soul coming alive. I can tell we will all work well together. Taking a deep breath, I try to soak up this moment. I'm honored that these people will be the ones standing behind me during this process.

As the meeting wraps up and everyone begins gathering their papers and laptops, I stand to address my team. "Before you all leave, I'd like to say a few words." The room quiets down.

"The dream team is finally together!" I grin and everyone chuckles. We have to add some humor and fun into this campaign or it will kill our souls. "This next year will be extremely busy and require a lot of hard work, but I'm confident that we can take on the challenge! I know tonight's meeting has been grueling since we are in the thick of finalizing my campaign strategy and confirming endorsements, but I'm beyond grateful to have you all here."

Everyone smiles and shakes my hand before leaving.

My excitement turns into dread as soon as I look over and notice Paul still sitting at the opposite end of the table. He always looks pretty serious, but he has been unusually quiet this evening. He looks up and meets my gaze as the last of our campaign team trickles out of the room. Once it's just David and I left, he finally speaks.

"Can I talk with you privately, Madden?"

I'm taken aback for a moment and glance at David. Paul knows I trust my brother implicitly. But, according to the sweat forming on his brow, he has horrible news to share. My stomach tightens.

I have dreamt of becoming a Congressman since I was in high school. That goal propelled me into law school and countless hours of volunteer work on political campaigns over the years since then. If this fails, it will devastate me. I'll have to continue working as a lawyer, which was never my long-term career plan.

Paul, David, and I stare at each other awkwardly for a few seconds before David stands from his chair and begins to exit the room to give us some privacy.

"Wait. No disrespect, Paul, but my brother is someone I confide everything in. Anything you need to say to me, you can say in front of David as well." I nervously run my hand through my wavy blonde hair.

"Very well."

Paul walks ahead of us, toward the armchairs by the fireplace. Once he's out of earshot, David whispers mockingly, "Somebody's in trouble." I try to give him a nonchalant smile, but I feel queasy.

"Have a seat, I'll try to make this as straightforward as possible." Paul motions to the two chairs in front of the fireplace and David and I lower ourselves into them a little uneasily. Paul is only looking at me now. I wish my parents hadn't lit the fire, because I can already feel sweat trickling down my back.

"Madden, you hired me because I'm good at what I do. You've watched me help several politicians get elected into office, and that's my hope for you as well. To prepare for our first meeting tonight, I've been studying past congressional representatives who served in Kansas. After scouring over the data these past few weeks, I have a few concerns."

Paul takes a deep breath. "If I didn't know how important this congressional campaign is to you, I might not even mention such a seemingly trivial issue, but..."

David and I look at each other nervously. I make a circling motion with my hand, urging Paul to continue.

"Kansas is a conservative, Republican state. Since you're running as a libertarian, you already have the odds against you. My research shows that every state representative before you was not only married, but had children as well. My point being, in contrast to congressmen before you, voters may see you as uncommitted and immature. Especially because you're much younger than anyone who has represented this state. I'm afraid they won't see you as someone who takes the needs of their families seriously."

He pauses and clears his throat, contemplating his words. "To put it bluntly, married individuals are much more likely to win the conservative vote. Kansas's voters want to see a family man who exudes strong morals and family values. *I* know you have the drive to serve your constituents, but I'm not confident that voters will see that."

Once Paul finishes, the room is eerily quiet. Even David's good humor has vanished, and his skin looks pale. None of us know what to say.

After a few seconds of processing, I'm able to take a deep breath and form words again. "But have there been any single men who have ran before? Most candidates are older and therefore happen to be married. But is it really a prerequisite?"

"There *have* been single men who have run before." Paul clears his throat. "They didn't win."

I cross my arms over my chest. "How do you know it was their *relationship status* that lost them the vote, though? Couldn't it have been a lack of supporters or a botched campaign?"

"Exit polls. A majority of voters who chose the married opponent reported they based their choice on his family situation."

I blink. "You're joking."

"Unfortunately, no, which proves my point: you'll look like a much stronger candidate if you have a supportive wife by your side. Especially since whoever runs against you will likely be much older and married with kids. Which will give them a leg up." Paul states with confidence.

My eyebrows shoot up. I know I must look befuddled, but I am having a hard time grasping what he's trying to say. Finally, I guffaw and say a little too loudly, "What am I supposed to do, Paul? Purchase a mail-order bride from Russia?"

I hear David snicker from the chair next to me, but after Paul shoots a glare in his direction, he quickly disguises the chuckle as a cough.

"I'm certain a Russian bride would not win over the American people, Madden. Try to take this seriously." Paul lets out a heavy, annoyed sigh. "Listen, you are a young, handsome man from a well-respected family. There must be a line of excellent young ladies trying to catch your eye. Or, if you're already seeing someone, now would be the perfect time to settle down."

"You're not seriously suggesting that I get married just for this political campaign, are you?" I take a moment to contemplate, but the longer I think about it, the hotter my anger boils inside of me. "All I want to do is get to Congress and help make positive change for the American people. And you're telling me the very people I want to help will doubt my motives just because there isn't a woman by my side?"

"You're upset. I understand. But you have to remember the demographics of Kansas's fourth district. Fifty-six percent of residents are married, and on average those married couples have two to three children. It's a near certainty that whoever runs against you will not only be married with children, but will also be a Republican. That means that, right off the bat, over half the population will identify more strongly with your opponent than with you." Paul comes around my chair and places his hand on my shoulder in a comforting gesture.

I take a deep breath. "This is ridiculous. I've lived in Kansas my entire life. I know the needs of the people here, not to mention that my father is a well-known orthopedic surgeon in the area and has secured a lot of supporters for me with his pull alone. But none of that matters if I don't have a ring on my finger?" When did I get transported back to the pioneer days?

Paul rubs his temples. "By your reaction, I assume you don't have a serious girlfriend?"

"No, Paul, I'm afraid I'm *very* single." I don't even attempt to hide my sarcasm.

David stands and begins pacing in front of the fireplace. "Okay, Madden, I know this isn't ideal, and I assume you haven't even entertained the idea of marriage since you and Jen broke up–"

I scoff, and David holds up his hands in acknowledgment. "Just go with me on this. What about... a marriage of convenience?"

I stare at David in utter confoundment. He must take my silence for approval because he continues. "I mean, arranged marriages–er, marriages of convenience–have been going on for centuries. Maybe this is just my logical CPA brain talking, but if we take romance out of the equation and just find a woman who holds the same values as you, we could make this work. And he has some time, right Paul?"

Paul perks up a bit. "Good point, David."

"What sane woman would agree to marry me on the fly?"

David's smile falters. "Well, we have time to figure that out."

Paul turns his attention back to me. "Do you remember the Nebraskan senator I was campaign manager for two years ago? He was much older than you, but he married the daughter of an influential man to gain supporters. They ended up falling in love and are extremely happy together today. It happens more than you'd think."

I scrub my hand down my face, exhausted by this conversation. I can almost feel my lifelong dreams slipping through my fingers. "This is madness. A marriage of convenience?"

"I'm sure it seems archaic, but this wouldn't be the first time a politician considered this kind of arrangement for political pull. Think of it as an alliance, like one country helping another," Paul offers.

Shaking my head back and forth, I stand. "I need some time to think about this."

David and Paul nod and say their goodbyes, but I hardly hear them. As I drive home to my apartment, feeling exasperated, I know that I'm in for the most sleepless night of my adult life.

⇜

I wake up the next morning feeling stiff and exhausted from tossing and turning all night. Deciding I need to focus on work instead of dwelling on my marital status, I walk to grab my laptop off my desk in the corner, but find it empty. I sigh. I must have left the laptop at my parent's house in my rush to leave last night.

I grab my wallet and shoot Mom a text, letting her know I'm on my way over.

Compared with bigger cities, Wichita's morning traffic is pretty mild, so I make it across town to College Hill quickly. After pulling my Audi into my parents' driveway, I walk across the yard and straight into their house without knocking. My parents tend to be on the formal side, but they have always made it clear to me and my three younger siblings that their door is always open to us.

Striding into the dining room, I see my parents sitting at opposite ends of the large dining table, as usual. Despite having the day off, my dad is wearing slacks and a long-sleeved dress shirt. His formerly blonde hair, now turned grey, is combed neatly to the side, and his blue eyes are focused on the newspaper in front of him. My mother, who also doesn't know the wonder that is sweat pants, is wearing a long-sleeved, crew-neck dress in a lilac color. She looks as lovely as ever, with her dark brown hair and high cheekbones.

"Good morning! Have some coffee if you want it." Dad looks up at me over his newspaper and pauses. "Well, you look awful. On second thought, please get yourself some coffee right away."

I roll my eyes. Coffee sounds incredible, though, so I make my way toward the kitchen. Tragically, Mom glances up from her Kindle as I pass her chair. "Oh, my. You *do* look terrible. I had assumed that your father was just being critical, as usual." She narrows her eyes at Dad, who expertly ignores her.

"I didn't sleep much last night." I run my fingers through my already messed up hair. "I'll tell you about it after I have some coffee. Maybe you two can help." My parents look confused but stay quiet until I return to the dining room a moment later with my steaming mug.

After taking a seat and savoring a few sips of my coffee in silence, Dad folds his newspaper and lays it to the side. "Okay, what can we help with?"

With a deep breath, I catch them up on my conversation with Paul and David from the night before, recanting the dilemma of my singleness and apparently needing a wife to get a seat in Congress.

When I finish, Dad furrows his brow. "That's preposterous. Does this Paul fellow even know what he's talking about?"

I grimace. "Yes. Paul emailed me the links to his research last night. I scrolled through some of it and it checks out."

Mom's eyes twinkle with delight, and I internally groan. She's been waiting for a good excuse to marry me off and plan a wedding, especially since my little sister Sophie eloped. "Well, we know plenty of lovely young ladies! Oh, just think of the wedding we could plan." She claps her hands together.

"Settle down, Diane." Dad barks at Mom from across the table. "There's no reason for any son of mine to marry someone if he doesn't want to."

I stand and walk over to the fireplace where I left my computer bag last night. After powering on my MacBook, I walk back over to my father and pull up Paul's email for him to look over. "I've been up all night thinking about this, and it doesn't look like anything will get me elected without a wife."

Dad busies himself scrolling through the links Paul sent while Mom grabs a notepad and starts writing a list of her friends' single daughters. I finish my cup of coffee and walk back into the kitchen to get a refill while my Dad stares at my computer with a stern brow. When I enter the dining room again, I see my mother is making a new Pinterest board–"Madden's Wedding"–on her phone.

Finally, Dad has read enough. He closes the laptop and folds his hands together. "Well, I suppose you need to decide how important it is to you to become a Congressman. How far are you willing to go?"

Mom sets her phone down and looks at me. "You have some time to date, right? I mean, you won't announce your campaign until mid-January."

"I suppose so..."

Dad scratches his chin, deep in thought. "Marriage seems extreme. Can't you simply fake an engagement? Then you could stage a break up after you're elected and everyone goes home happy."

"An engagement doesn't really scream *committed family man*, now does it? People end engagements all the time. Marriage would make him look much more serious, Ted." Mom shoots Dad an indignant look, then continues. "It's the end of May already, so realistically you'd want to be engaged by October." She calculates the months on her fingers.

"October seems fast." I draw in a shaky breath.

"The timeline isn't ideal, but people have met and gotten married in far less time, right?"

"I wouldn't say that's a ringing endorsement," Dad mutters into his coffee as he takes a sip.

I slump in my chair. "I've worked so hard for this. At the end of the day, I think I'm willing to do whatever it takes to get to Congress."

"If this is really what you want to do..." Dad frowns in disapproval, then heaves a gusty, resigned sigh. "Well, it's not like the marriage *has* to last forever."

Mom's jaw drops. "Don't put that idea in his head!"

But Dad's comment has planted a seed in my thoughts. "He's not wrong. What if I could find a girl who would be willing to marry me for just a few years?"

"Madden!" Mom looks between Dad and I in horror.

Dad smiles slowly, probably because he knows he's making my mother fume. "You know, several of my friends have a marriage clause in their daughter's trust funds. I'd be willing to bet that one of those girls might be willing to marry you just to get their hands on their trust money."

Mom purses her lips at my dad, then turns her head toward me. "Madden, think of the scandal if word got out! It would ruin your chances of getting elected!"

I nod, conceding the point. But I have an answer for it. "Don't most people sign prenups before getting married? We could just throw in a non-disclosure agreement as well."

"But will a woman like that make a good politician's wife? You need someone poised and proper by your side." Mom rips her list of eligible ladies from the notepad and shakes it toward me. "*These* are the type of women who will get you to Congress."

"Will one of those women agree to marry me in four months and be willing to dissolve the marriage after I get elected?"

Mom throws up her hands and looks frantically at Dad. "Ted, tell your son he's being irrational."

Dad purses his lips thoughtfully. "Your mother has a point. You'll probably need to meet a few of these trust fund babies first and see if you can find one who'll be an asset to your campaign."

I grin back at him. "You're brilliant."

Mom stomps out of the room, mumbling something about not wanting anything to do with our villainous plans.

I focus my attention back to my Dad. "Would it really be so horrible? As long as the woman got something out of the marriage as well? I'll get my seat in Congress, she'll get her trust fund."

"It's not an ideal situation, obviously. Whether it's for two years or fifty, marriage is a big commitment." Dad glances tiredly at the door my mother just stormed through. "But if you really want to do this, I can get you a list of names."

"Yes. I want to do this. Get me a list and I'll go on dates until I find one suitable enough." I scratch my chin as I think. "It can't be just anyone, she'll have to play the part of a doting wife *and* be intelligent enough to win over the public."

My father smirks. "And be pleasant enough for you to live with for a few years?"

I throw my head back with a groan. "Ugh, this already sounds impossible. But I have to at least try."

Chapter 1

Odette

♥

My flight lands in Wichita on a hot August evening, and everything looks wonderfully familiar. Dwight D. Eisenhower Airport is my first reality of being home. Closing my eyes, I take a deep breath and I'm almost positive that I already smell the wheat, cows, sunflowers, and all the Kansas things.

I know that's impossible, but a girl can pretend.

I never thought I'd move back home at twenty-eight years old, but my dad's recent stroke made it imperative. I couldn't leave my mom to take care of him on her own. It's my duty as their only child to be there for my parents like they were always there for me. And I missed them terribly while I was in D.C. Having a job I loved didn't replace the feeling of family and community I left behind in Kansas.

With a smile on my face, I walk down the long hallway leading toward the exit. As I get close to the end of the hallway, though, a familiar voice calls to me.

"ODETTE!"

I swivel at the sound and see Kate waving at me from outside the security exit. I run to her and wrap her in a ridiculous embrace, both of us giggling and spinning in circles in the middle of the airport. A few people nearby stare at us, the two crazy women acting like little girls, but I don't care. I haven't seen my best friend in over a year.

My eyes become watery the moment Kate wraps her arms around me. Her hug feels like home. There is simply nothing that compares to the bond of a childhood friend–a friend I grew up with, who knows everything about me.

"Oh, my gosh, it's so good to see you!" I step back to get a better view of her.

Kate looks basically the same as she did when we were teens, though a prettier, adult version now. Her dark curly hair is much shorter than it was the last time I saw her. I didn't realize she got a pixie cut, but it looks exceptional, especially as it accentuates the ornery twinkle in her enormous hazel eyes.

But then I notice her dress and I can barely disguise the laugh that escapes from my mouth. "Kate, you know I love you, but what on earth are you wearing?"

She just giggles. "I want to be the most unforgettable teacher my students ever have. When they tell their children and their grandchildren about high school, I want them to say, 'Mrs. Augustine was the most vivacious, creative, and inspiring teacher I ever had!' So, naturally, I've been dressing like Miss Frizzle from *The Magic School Bus*!" She twirls around in her 1950s-style dress festooned with a colorful insect print.

"Miss Frizzle taught small children. You're a biology teacher at a private high school."

"Oh, you're no fun. Quit *bugging* me about my amazing dress." She erupts into laughter.

I shake my head, but I suppress an amused smile. Kate has always cracked herself up and I love her for it, even though she can be so over the top sometimes.

"I know you're jealous of my dress, but don't worry. I'll get one for you." Kate takes my carry-on bag and slips it onto her shoulder. "Actually, I would've changed before I picked you up, but we're going to be late to the reunion as it is."

I groan. "I can't believe I let you talk me into going to our high school reunion."

"Oh, stop. It'll be fun! Plus, we can see who's aging well and who's still single!" Kate waggles her eyebrows suggestively.

"I don't know, and I don't really care," I say as we walk to the escalator. "If I didn't want to date them in high school, I'm pretty sure I won't want to date them now."

"I wonder if Madden will be there. I saw him a few months ago and, let me tell you something, he is somehow even more gorgeous than he was ten years ago. And unlike most guys our age, he still has all of his hair." If a heart-eye emoji could take human form, it would look like Kate's face right now.

At the mention of Madden Windell, I feel a blush creep up my neck. I always thought he was extremely handsome, but he never paid any attention to me. I'm pretty sure, in fact, that he never knew I existed. We moved in very different social circles.

I feign a stumble at the bottom of the escalator, so hopefully Kate doesn't see my blush. I scoff in pretend disgust. "You're a happily married woman. Why on earth are you ogling Madden Windell? He always seemed like an airhead to me. He was so busy playing football, I'm not sure how he had any time to study."

"I wasn't looking at him for *me*. I was looking at him for my lovely, very single best friend, who just so happens to be moving back to the same city Madden lives in." Kate says, as we reach the baggage claim.

"I have barely stepped off the plane and you are already trying to marry me off! And to someone who would never even look twice at me." I step forward and search for my suitcase amongst the sea of bags rotating through the carousel.

I hear Kate mutter something under her breath about how I need to have a little fun. Then she sighs loudly. "Okay, I'll stop pestering you, I promise! I just adore you and want you to be happy, you know that, right?"

"Yes, of course I do," I say over my shoulder, spotting my plain black suitcase coming toward me. I grab it off the conveyor belt and we walk toward the exit, Kate looping her arm through mine.

"You really shouldn't pack so many books. Your carry-on must be well over the weight limit." She shifts my bag on her shoulder as we walk to the parking garage.

Playfully, I wink and nudge her hip with my own. "I only packed the important ones, of course."

She laughs as she unlocks her Jeep, then unceremoniously tosses my heavy carry-on into the back. "So, how do you feel about stopping for a drink and being *extra* late to the reunion?"

I hoist my suitcase into the back of her Jeep. "Yes, please! The later we arrive, the less small talk I have to make with former classmates."

We hop in the car and, with a smirk in my direction, Kate puts on Taylor Swift's "Welcome To New York", our go-to song whenever we get together. When we were younger, we had dreamt of leaving Wichita and living in a big city. Kate quickly put that dream aside after meeting her husband. Even though I eventually landed my fancy job in D.C., I can't help but feel a bit jealous of her.

Kate and I pull into a gas station and she runs inside to grab some boxed wine. While she's gone, I can't help but wonder if I'll see Madden tonight.

I shake my head, irritated that I even considered the thought. He probably doesn't even know who I am. The only class we had together was debate. I still remember his effortless speeches and confident charisma. His easy charm infuriated me at the time, since I struggled with confidence so much. Though most of the kids at my high school came from wealthy families, I could only attend via a scholarship program. Pair that with frizzy hair and knobby knees and you have a perfect specimen of a wallflower.

Kate jumps back into the vehicle, interrupting my thoughts. Trying to distract myself from thinking of my old crush from high school, I blurt, "So how are Jarod and the girls doing?"

Kate looks in her rearview mirror as she backs out of the parking spot. "Good! He really likes his job at Boeing. We're just hoping they don't have any more layoffs. And the girls love Heartland Academy. It's so nice to have them at my school now so I don't have to worry about childcare anymore. They absolutely adore their kindergarten teacher, and I get to eat lunch with them."

Kate looks genuinely happy, and I smile even as I try to ignore the longing that clenches my stomach. She got married right out of college to an amazing man and had twins a year later. Of course I'm happy for her. She's my closest friend and I want nothing but the best for her. But the pang of jealousy is still there.

Maybe someday I will find what she has.

"How's your Dad doing?" Kate asks sympathetically.

I pause, trying to hold back the tears that come so easily these days. "He is doing okay, I think. His memory just isn't the same. When I call him, he knows who I am but forgets my name. And also directions. He can't do anything alone, which gets overwhelming for my mom." My voice breaks with emotion. I glance out the window, trying to compose myself. "Sorry, it's difficult to talk about."

Kate puts her hand on my knee as she drives. "I'm so sorry. Your parents must be absolutely over the moon that you'll be here with them, though Moving back home was the best decision you could've made."

I put my hand on top of hers. "Thanks. It'll definitely be nice to see them every day."

"Do you have any plans now that you're back in town? I know you want to spend time with your parents, but do you think you'll look for part-time work or anything?"

I scrunch up my nose, unsure what to say. "Honestly, for the first time in my life, I don't have a plan, which stresses me out. I'm going from working as a legislative assistant to being unemployed. I'd like to find part-time work, but with a degree in political science, I'm not exactly sure what that would look like here in Wichita."

Kate knows me well enough that I'm sure she senses the sadness and anxiety in my voice. It was always impossible to hide my feelings from her. She gives my leg a gentle squeeze and then returns her hand to the steering wheel. "You gave up your dream career to move back, which shows how selfless you are. Good things will happen for you, I can just feel it."

I bashfully wave her comments away, but she continues. "Odette, I know you feel more at ease when you have a plan, but I want you to know that it's okay to not have one."

Somehow I manage a smile, even though my mind is reeling. Having a plan and preparing for the future *does* put my mind at ease. I had a plan two months ago, but since my dad's stroke, I don't know what the future holds anymore. With no other siblings to share the burden, I don't even want to imagine what my life will look like once my parents are gone.

Kate gives me an empathetic look and pats my shoulder. She pulls into the school parking lot, swinging into an empty space near the front of the building, then grabs the boxed wine and two paper cups. Alcohol isn't allowed inside the school, but it's fine by me to enjoy our drinks in the peace and quiet of the parking lot, anyway.

Just as I take my first sip, "Rewrite The Stars" from *The Greatest Showman* comes on the radio. We look at each other with our mouths agape. The radio fairies knew we needed this exact song. Naturally, we break out into our own little concert.

Chapter 2

Madden

♥

Trying to leave work on time on a Friday is nearly impossible. Christopher Highman, my power-hungry coworker who unfortunately made partner last week, has become even more conceited than he was before.

At first glance, he seems like a nice guy with his blue eyes, curly brown hair, and rosy cheeks. But despite his handsome face, he's incredibly rude to everyone around him. His only redeeming quality is that his clients adore him. The man is a savage in the courtroom.

Working at Bennington and Associates hasn't been all bad, though. I've actually enjoyed working with Richard Bennington, and the building itself is gorgeous. Our downtown office was designed to impress, and it has to since we serve the wealthiest clients in the area. Sleek furniture fills glass-walled offices and pricey artwork adorns the halls. My favorite part, though, is our view of the Wichita skyline. It's not as grand as New York City, but Wichita is home.

Just as I'm logging off my computer to head home, the devil himself glides into my office with a smirk and lifts a large pile of folders in his hands. "Madden, you weren't leaving already, were you?"

I glance at my watch. "Well, it's six o'clock on a Friday, so yes. Yes, I was."

He drops the pile onto my desk with a loud *thwack*. "Ahh, I see. I guess that's why one of us made partner sooner."

Taking a deep breath, I casually thumb through some of the files, reminding myself that Robert wanted to offer *me* the partner position, but I asked him not to since I'm leaving the firm in a few months to run for Congress. And wouldn't that wipe the smirk off Christopher's face. I shrug. "True. You're just a much harder worker than me. But why did you bring me these files? Your paralegal will deal with them."

"Despite your tendency to go home early, you're better at prepping court appeals than Sarah." He rolls his eyes. "Richard and I are working on an important case for our biggest client, and everything needs to be flawless."

With a deep sigh, I rest my hands on my hips. "I'm not doing your grunt work, Christopher. Sarah is an extremely competent paralegal. You can leave these with her."

Richard Bennington himself suddenly pops his head into my office. Just in time. "What are you guys still doing here? Go home!" He smiles, then notices the large stack of files. "What are those?"

My eyes shift to Christopher. Judging by the vacant smile on his face, he knows he's been caught in his obnoxious attempt to make me do busywork.

"Well, Christopher was just telling me I should take care of these before I leave."

Richard's head whips around to look at Christopher. "Being a partner doesn't mean you can force Madden to do your paperwork. Take those to Sarah. And I'll see you both on Monday."

Richard walks away just before Christopher sends me a death glare and dramatically scoops up his files. As he leaves, I walk across the room and close the door, grab a casual polo shirt from my briefcase, and change out of my dress shirt and tie. Tucking in my polo, I take a quick glance at the small mirror on my office wall and give myself an internal pep talk.

Okay, Madden, time to go on another date. I know this is the 12th date in two months, but It's only for one hour. Then you can duck out early to speak at your high school reunion.

With a groan, I leave the office and drive to the restaurant.

As I park my car at the Italian restaurant my date chose, I spot a young woman by the entrance, watching me. I've never met Heidi before, but the moment I spot her I know she's my date. She looks exactly like every other woman from my dad's list: skinny, blonde, obvious breast implants, a designer handbag, and four-inch-heels.

A week after speaking to my parents about my marriage dilemma, Dad gave me a list of women with a marriage clause in their trust funds–as far as he knew, at least. However, after twelve dates–thirteen after tonight–they had all proven themselves to be nothing but spoiled daddy's girls, clacking around in their stilettos and unable to talk about anything other than their travels and spa retreats. None of these women would make me look good in the public eye. Instead, they'd frame me as just another slimy, money-hungry politician.

I'm probably being too hard on Heidi. I haven't even spoken to her yet. Maybe she'll break the mold.

"Oh, you must be Madden! You look just like your Facebook photo." She beams at me, then reaches down to pet her purse. Wait, no... there's a dog *inside* her purse.

Dear Lord, please help this hour go by fast.

Trying not to stare at the purse dog, I look directly at her face. "Yes, pleased to meet you, Heidi."

She giggles. "And don't forget Pompom!"

I clear my throat and force myself to look at the dog. "Right, good evening... Pompom." Opening the door for her, I gesture for her to walk inside. "Like I mentioned over the phone, I only have an hour. My high school reunion is tonight."

I tack on that last part for good measure, hoping it sounds convincing. I could be late to my reunion, of course, but I have a feeling I won't want this date to go over one hour.

She walks through the door, grabbing my arm with her free hand as she passes. "Oh, that's okay. I have a nail appointment after this, anyway."

The hostess seats us at our table in a private room and we spend the next agonizing hour talking about the chain of luxury condos her father owns. Trying not to be too obvious, I glance down at my watch every five minutes, but she's too preoccupied with her dog to notice.

Not soon enough. The hour is over. I pay the bill and we amicably go our separate ways. I get in my car and scrub one exhausted hand down my face. I'm beginning to sweat this whole marriage thing. There are only five women left on my dad's list, and if they're anything like their thirteen predecessors, not a single one of them will be suitable. After all this time and stress, will I *still* have to give up my congressional goals?

As I drive over to my old high school, I try to relax by pushing away thoughts of the campaign and instead thinking back to what my life was like ten years ago. Honestly, I don't mind these silly reunions because I have a lot of great memories from high school. I remember being surrounded by friends, playing football, having no responsibilities, and never having trouble getting a date.

Thinking of dating invites a fresh wave of nerves. I'll probably have to see my ex-fiancée tonight, since Jen and I went to high school together. She lives in Wichita, so I assume she'll be there. My heart is racing and my stomach feels unsettled.

When I finally reach the school parking lot, I put my car in park and take a deep breath. After a few minutes, I walk inside.

I take in the tile flooring and scuffed, off-white walls, which still look exactly the same. I can smell the lemony scent of the cleaner our janitor, Mr. Holcomb, used every day. I swear I even detect a hint of the aroma of the pizza they served for lunch every Friday–which is why Fridays were always my favorite day of the week.

I never imagined I'd be back at Heartland Academy ten years later, but the class president is supposed to give a brief speech. And I was, of course, the class president. It's definitely cheesy, but now that I'm starting my campaign, I need to get used to making public appearances. This will be good practice.

As I walk into the gymnasium, I hear music and the merry chatter of my former classmates. Someone took a lot of time decorating the gym with gold- and navy-colored streamers and balloons, our school colors.

I forget my nerves about seeing Jen when I spot half a dozen of my old football teammates standing in a circle by the drink table. They wave me over with broad grins.

"Hey, guys! Good to see you!" I smile as we all exchange fist bumps. They all look pretty much the same. Most of the guys have lost their youthful chub, but we're only twenty-eight. It's not like we've all gotten' grey and wrinkly yet.

"Dude, what have you been up to? Still working as a lawyer?" My old friend, Greg, asks. He still looks exactly the same, his muscular build dressed in a t-shirt and gym shorts with his shaggy black hair falling into his eyes.

I casually cross my arms over my chest. "Yes, but only for a few more weeks. I'm running for Congress in the next election."

"Congrats! Obviously, you have my vote. Anyone who can lead a football team like you did can probably lead our state, too." The man speaking shrugs. I can't remember his name. Ten years suddenly feels like a long time.

The guys continue talking around me, but their voices fade and my body goes numb as my eyes suddenly lock with Jennifer Briar-

Keebler's across the room. She looks as beautiful as ever with her long, blonde hair, blue eyes, and tight, royal-blue dress. I try not to notice her dress's much-too-revealing neckline and the way her legs look in her sky-high heels. Good thing Principal Jenkins isn't here. Her dress is definitely against Heartland's dress code.

My stomach clenches and it feels difficult to swallow. This is the moment I've been dreading since the school called and asked me to speak. I no longer have feelings for her, but the pang of hurt is still there. Jen and I were just friends in high school, but when we attended the same law school, we started dating. I fell head over heels in love with her, and we got engaged shortly after graduation. Jen then proceeded to string me along for a four-year engagement before breaking up with me a year ago, stating that she found my political aspirations overwhelming.

I brace myself as I see her walking towards me. How does she walk in those heels?

Greg notices her coming towards us as well. "I heard about the breakup. Sorry, man. If I'd ever been lucky enough to have a woman who looks like that, I know I'd still be pining after her." He shakes his head, ogling Jen.

I give his shoulder a pat. "There's more to women than just their looks. Even the most beautiful woman can make you miserable. You'd be surprised."

He grins, still watching Jen. "I'd like the chance to find out for myself."

I roll my eyes. Some people have to learn the hard way.

"Madden, good to see you." Jen stops in front of me with a tight smile. "I wasn't sure if you'd be here tonight."

My shoulders tense up as I give her an awkward grin that probably looks more like a grimace. "Good to see you too, Jen. Where's Bryan?" I try to sound casual as I inquire about the man she left me for.

Jen takes a deep breath, appearing annoyed. "Oh, he went to get us some punch."

"Well, well, well! If it isn't Madden Windell!" I hear the unmistakable, annoying voice of my former friend and law school roommate coming from behind me. "I can't believe you're not busy tonight doing fancy lawyer stuff." He scoffs bitterly as he hands Jen her drink.

I can't suppress my smirk. Bryan was never able to pass the Bar Exam and he must still be sour about it. He really hasn't changed much in the past year, except his midsection might have become pudgier. His light-brown hair looks the same, along with his shifty brown eyes.

"You finally ready to run for Congress?" Bryan asks, attempting to jut his non-existent chest muscles out.

He seems awfully arrogant for a used car salesman, but what do I know? I resist the urge to groan and respond with my most charming smile. "Actually, I'm running in the next election, thank you for asking."

"Oh, that's wonderful! We wish you the best of luck with your campaign! Don't we, Bryan?" Jen glares at her husband as she nudges him with her elbow.

Bryan simply nods, and one side of his mouth curves up into a smile. Or maybe it's a sneer.

Jen's eyes dart between the two of us and she laughs nervously, like she thinks the two of us are about to brawl with each other. She doesn't need to worry about that, though. I'd never waste a good punch on a scumbag like Bryan Keebler.

Thankfully, I'm saved from any more awkward conversation when our former class secretary, Dana, appears at my side.

"Madden! There you are. Is this a good time for you to welcome everyone and say a few words?" She smiles awkwardly, perhaps sensing the weirdness she just interrupted. Dana is maybe five feet tall and has unruly brown hair. She was always kind and friendly back in high school, and I always enjoyed working together on class projects.

"Hey! Yeah, I can do that now. Is there a mic somewhere?"

She points to the small stage at the side of the gym. "The mic is turned on, so head up there whenever you're ready."

I'm so ready to get away from Jen and Bryan, so I offer a tense smile, excuse myself, and walk straight over to the stage. Public speaking comes naturally to me, so I'm not nervous at all. Instead, I feel amped up and energetic. As I walk confidently onto the stage, the football team cheers, which brings everyone's attention to me.

I grab the mic off the stand and shout, "Welcome, class of 2009!"

The crowd erupts in cheers again, and I grin. "I'd like to take a moment to thank you all for coming out tonight. Also, can we give Dana a round of applause for putting this reunion together?" Everyone erupts and chants Dana's name. I spot her in the crowd, blushing in embarrassment.

"In the last ten years, I'm sure we've all had unique experiences. Maybe our lives went as planned, or perhaps we were thrown a few unexpected trials. Either way, I hope we all have grown through it and have become better people than we were a decade ago."

I pause to smile at my old classmates, but an unexpected person comes into my line of sight, and she's... stunning. My entire body feels warm as her penetrating gaze meets mine, and for a few seconds, I forget that I'm on stage in front of a hundred people. All I see is her lovely face and lustrous red hair.

Who is she?

I blink a few times, realizing that I've lost my place in my speech. This never happens to me. I'm not sure what to do. Closing my eyes for a second, the words come back to me.

"Anyway, it's great to see you all, and I hope we'll have a wonderful evening catching up with old friends. And when we come back together for our twenty-year reunion, I'm eager to see how we'll have grown and matured even more. Thank you!"

Everyone claps as I exit the stage. I glance around the room, looking for the mysterious woman, but it's more difficult to find her now that I'm not on the stage. As I'm looking around, I spy Jen and Bryan in a corner arguing. Yikes. That can't be good.

With a bit of surprise, I realize I couldn't care less what they're arguing about. I breathe a sigh of relief. Deep down, I think I needed to prove to myself that I could be around them without feeling like my chest was going to cave in. Seeing them tonight was nothing compared to when I saw them last year after Jen broke up with me. I hope Bryan isn't an awful husband. Or, at least, I *want* to feel that way. My heart has a little ways to go, apparently.

I stick around for a bit, catching up with old friends and hoping to run into the gorgeous red-head, but I never see her again. She must be someone's wife. She definitely wasn't in my graduating class, or I'm sure I would've remembered her.

Exiting the gym, I walk back down the long hallway to get back to the front parking lot. Standing on the stairs in front of the school, I take a moment to enjoy the brilliant Kansas sunset on this hot August evening. They're always glorious and full of brilliant pinks and blues, like swirling cotton candy. Inhaling the humid summer air, I smile to myself.

Suddenly, I hear a strange crumpling noise to my left. I turn my head to investigate.

When I glance over my shoulder, I see *her,* the mysterious redhead. She's sitting on a step on the other side of the wide staircase. She gracefully tosses her wavy red hair over her shoulder as she rummages through her handbag. When she looks up, she holds a stick of gum in front of her and whispers triumphantly, "Ah, there you are."

"Are you speaking to your gum?" I ask, and she jumps. She must have been so immersed in her quest for gum that she didn't realize anyone else had come outside.

She blushes–which I find adorable–then meets my gaze with her forest-green eyes. "Oh! I'm sorry, Madden, I didn't see you there."

Does she know me? My thoughts spin. Surely I would've remembered meeting this lovely creature. She looks like a majestic fae escaped from some fantasy novel. And I don't even read fantasy.

"I'm sorry, do we know each other?" I think for a moment, trying to place her. "Were you in my graduating class?"

She furrows her eyebrows and slides her purse onto her shoulder, seemingly annoyed. "Oh. Nope. I just know your name since you gave the speech earlier."

I walk over and reach my hand out. "It's a pleasure to meet you, Miss..." I pause, hoping she'll tell me her name.

A smirk crosses her lips for just a moment before she gently shakes my hand and responds with an amused twinkle in her eye, "My friends call me Red."

Taking advantage of the opportunity, I glance down at our hands and don't see a ring on her finger. Excellent.

"Well, I can see why." I wink. I hold onto her hand longer than necessary and give her my best smolder. Flynn Rider mixed with Chris Hemsworth. "So who are you here with, *Red*?"

She pulls her hand out of mine and bites her bottom lip. After thinking for a few seconds, she slowly answers, "Um... my boyfriend. Greg."

I raise an eyebrow. The fact that she had to think about it tells me she's lying. But why would anyone lie about such a trivial thing, especially to a stranger? "Really? I'm good friends with Greg. I spoke with him earlier, but he never mentioned a girlfriend."

Her lovely, heart-shaped mouth makes a "tsk" sound. "Well! I can't believe him. I better go have a chat. With Greg."

"Right. Nice meeting you, Red."

"Er, yes. Nice meeting you too, Madden."

Before I can utter another word, she turns on her heel and scuttles back inside, leaving me completely befuddled. And intrigued.

Chapter 3

Odette

♥

I wake up the next morning in my childhood bedroom. As I take in the room, it's obvious that Mom and Dad never moved a thing from its place since I left for college years ago. My twin bed feels comfortable and familiar, complete with the pink comforter I received for my 16th birthday. I run my hand over the fluffy matching pillow and give an extra hug to Mr. Rexy, my sparkly T-Rex.

Note to self: redecorate my bedroom before I begin sleeping with all of my stuffed animals on the regular.

Thinking back to last night at the reunion, my face grows hot remembering my strange interaction with Madden. I know we weren't close in high school, but he didn't even know who I was. I huff a frustrated breath. Oh, well. I probably won't see him again anytime soon. Why waste valuable brain cells thinking about teenage fantasies?

Suddenly, I get a whiff of my Mom's infamous cinnamon rolls drifting through the door. Is there a better scent in the entire world? I think not. The mouthwatering smell is enough to pull me from my bed–and Mr. Rexy.

I grab my robe and slippers from my suitcase and walk out to the kitchen where my sweet mom is busy cleaning up the mess from her baking and humming along to oldies on the radio.

Despite all the stress since Dad's stroke, she looks well. Her wavy, grey hair is cut adorably short, and she's wearing her signature outfit: a cardigan, simple khaki pants, and her floral apron. But what always stands out the most is her bright, contagious smile.

I experience the full wattage of that smile when she turns, spotting me.

I rush across the kitchen and wrap my arms around her. "Oh, Mom! It's so good to be home! And those cinnamon rolls smell amazing!"

She pulls back and looks me over. "Odette, you look wonderful! A little thin, but we'll fix that in no time. I'm sorry we were already asleep by the time Kate brought you home last night. I'm afraid we go to bed pretty early these days."

"No problem! I was jet-lagged, anyway. Besides, I'm here to take care of you and Dad, not the other way around. So stop spoiling me and teach me your baking secrets."

"Nonsense. What will I do with myself if I can't spoil my only child?" She grins. "Your dad is excited to see you. He's in the living room."

I smile and head in Dad's direction. Their old house is small, with a rounded doorway separating each room. As I walk through the kitchen and into the living room, I see him relaxing in his recliner. He's watching the morning news, like he does every morning, but he turns toward me when he hears my footsteps.

His face crinkles up in a smile, making the wrinkles on his weathered face stand out. "How's my baby girl?"

My heart squeezes. I can't help but wonder if he called me "baby girl" because he struggles with names these days. Either way, I accept the endearment.

"It's so good to be back." I walk forward to his chair and bend down to give him a hug so he won't need to stand. When I pull back, I can't help but get a little choked up. He's aged so much this past year, looking closer to eighty-five years old than his actual seventy-five.

His eyes are sunken and the skin on his face sags from all the weight he has lost. I can tell how hard his body and mind took the stroke.

I glance once at the droning TV and then place my hands on my hips. "Watching the news again, I see. Do you want me to make some coffee?"

He lifts one ornery brow. "Alright, but try not to make it too weak this time." He winks and then breaks into a laugh.

I chuckle. It's so good to hear him tease and laugh. There was a time when I worried he would never laugh again. "Hilarious. We both know I make the best coffee in this family."

"Coffee isn't supposed to resemble tea, Odette."

"I do not make weak coffee!" I turn on my heel. "I'll be right back with the most amazing cup of coffee you've ever tasted."

As I walk back into the kitchen, I note with a smile that the house looks exactly the same. Mom's decorating tastes haven't changed a bit. There's an apple-printed tablecloth with matching curtains at the window, identical hand towels, and even an apple-shaped soap dispenser by the sink. Only my mother could make so many apple items somehow look adorable.

She looks up from scrubbing dishes as I come to stand beside her. "It seems like Dad is doing really well today. He wants his morning coffee. Do you still keep the coffee beans above the microwave?"

"Yes, in the cupboard. And please try not to make the coffee too weak this time. You know how he hates that."

I catch the twinkle in her eye and burst out laughing. "I can tell you've been conspiring with Dad. Maybe I should just get you two a coffee subscription."

She huffs out a short laugh, but then her face takes on a more serious expression. "I know you haven't been home since... well, since your dad's health took a turn. But I have his medication and therapy schedule written on the calendar." She nods to the calendar hung by the fridge. "That way you'll know what's going on each day."

"You know how I like to be organized." I stride across the room to look at the schedule. "I'm sorry you've been doing this all alone. I gave my notice at work as soon as I got out of my lease."

"It's alright. I'm just glad that you're here now. I hate that you had to give up your job to move home, though." She nudges her shoulder against mine in apology, and I nudge her back. "Oh, and before I forget, the Buick in the garage still runs. I know it's not the fanciest car, but it's there if you need it."

"Oh, that's sweet of you." I offer a reassuring smile, trying not to grimace at the thought of driving my parents' old Buick around town. That thing is the definition of a beater car. "And listen, I loved my job, but it's not like I was leaving close friends behind. All I did was work, work, and more work."

"But what about the nice man you were seeing? I know long-distance wouldn't be ideal, but we'd love to see you settle down with a good man." Mom tries to sound nonchalant, suddenly busying herself drying a mixing bowl with her dishcloth.

"I haven't had my morning coffee yet and you're already bringing up my love life?" I set to work making the coffee and try not to let on how flustered her comment leaves me. The men I met in D.C. were career-focused and driven. They enjoyed dating in their spare time, but once they realized I wasn't down to just *have a good time*, they quickly put me off. I usually tried not to let it bother me, but it stung today.

"And besides, I wasn't *seeing* a man in D.C. Two dates hardly builds enough foundation for a long-distance relationship. Plus, that guy was kind of a jerk." I don't bother explaining to Mom that we stopped dating because he wanted more than a peck on the cheek at the end of our second date.

"Alright. I'm sorry for bringing it up. I would just love grandchildren before I get too much older." She gives me a side-long glance.

"Between you and Kate, I'm sure I'll be married off in no time. Plus, we all know how men like a single, book-loving, old maid like myself."

"Oh, brother." She rolls her eyes. "Listen here, daughter of mine. You inherited my beautiful auburn hair and your father's emerald green eyes. Not to mention that you have the work ethic of a draft horse and the organizational skills of a hive of bees. Who could resist you?"

"I think you just described a secretary. You should write that in my online dating profile, though. Men will line up at our door."

"Oh, of course. Should I also post the photo I took of you this morning, snuggled up asleep with Mr. Rexy?" She snaps back with a completely straight face.

I am equal parts horrified and impressed. "You wouldn't. Especially if you actually want someone to marry me and give you grandchildren."

We break into giggles, when suddenly Dad yells from the other room, "Would you two quit the chatter and bring me a cup of Odette's weak coffee?"

Chapter 4

Madden

♥

I step out of my Audi into the cool November air, leaves rustling around my feet as I walk into George's Bistro in downtown Wichita. My mom and brothers invited me to lunch and, as much as I love excellent food, I can't help but dread this meeting. They probably want to interrogate me about my total failure.

I was supposed to have found a woman and proposed to her by now, but after going out with the nearly twenty women that my dad recommended over the past four months, I still have found no one I'd be willing to marry, even for just a few years. I even scrolled through all of my contacts multiple times and considered reaching out to a few old flames, but I thought better of it. How could I expect any rational woman to enter a fake marriage with me if she won't receive any benefit? At least the trust fund babies would have gotten some money.

How will I get to Congress now?

I strike my fist against my thigh. The only woman I felt any connection with in the past few months was the stunning redhead I met at my high school reunion in August. And every day I internally kick myself for not getting her number. Maybe she would've been the answer to my problems.

I'm sure my brothers will have some practical advice for me, although I wouldn't call them marriage experts. David never dates and Brooks dates too much.

After the hostess seats me, I order a charcuterie plate–since Mom loves it so much– and lean back in my chair to take in my surroundings. George's Bistro is a little piece of Paris in Wichita. With the black walls, gold trim, and modern gold sconces, the aesthetics are remarkable and the food is incredible. I close my eyes and take a deep breath. It feels good to enjoy a moment of peace after such a hectic week.

When I open my eyes again, I see my brothers walking toward me. So much for peace.

Standing to greet them, I notice with suspicion that they both have huge, mischievous grins on their faces. We all take our seats and Brooks picks up the menu to study it, concealing his face. David simply smiles innocently.

"Okay, what's going on? Why do you both look so suspicious?"

David sniffs. "I don't know what you're talking about."

Just as I'm about to call him out on his bald-faced lie, Brooks drops his menu and confesses. "Okay, okay. Don't be dramatic! Sheesh. You know the Hastings, that older couple from church that Mom and Dad adopted as their own little charity case?"

"Yeah? What about them?" I look between my brothers in confusion.

"Do you remember that they have a daughter, Odette? She went to high school with you." Brooks raises his eyebrows suggestively.

"Odette Hastings?" Her name sounds vaguely familiar. "She might have been on my debate team. She was pretty quiet, though. I remember little about her."

"So, a few days ago, David and I met for dinner and we saw Mom at the same restaurant, eating with Mrs. Hastings. Well, Odette stopped in to pick up her mom and *whoa*." Brooks says dramatically, eyes opened wide.

David nods in agreement and looks at me like I should know what they're talking about.

"*Whoa*, what?" I ask in irritation.

"*Whoa*, meaning she looks a lot different than she did in high school. She's kind of a babe now." David laces his fingers together in front of him and smirks.

I chuckle. "We can't possibly be thinking of the same person. The girl on my debate team wasn't very attractive, from what I can remember."

Brooks scoffs. "I'm not old like you two, so I never saw her in high school, but the woman we saw was gorgeous."

"What is the point of this conversation, anyway?" I ask with one eyebrow raised.

Brooks throws his head back in exasperation. "She could be the perfect wife for you! Keep up."

With my face void of expression and my tone dripping with sarcasm, I respond slowly, "Really? And she's willing to sign away the next two years of her life just to help me win my campaign? Come on."

Brooks goes on, undeterred. "She looked like the perfect Congressman's wife. And she had a kind smile, unlike all those women Dad suggested."

"There's no way we're talking about the same person." I scrunch my nose up. "And you never met those women. How do you know what they looked like?"

Brooks' expression freezes in a caught-red-handed smile. "I might have peeked at Dad's list and called up a few... Only after you nixed them, though!"

David cuts in, probably hoping to avoid an argument. "Look, Madden, would it really hurt to get to know her? You might have more in common than you think. We asked Mom about her and she says Odette just moved back from D.C. Maybe she's into the whole congressman thing."

This conversation is ruining my appetite, which is unacceptable. I haven't had my crème brûlée yet. "Guys, she could be the greatest thing since indoor plumbing and it still wouldn't matter. She's not going to go for a *marriage of convenience*. Besides, if she's so great, why hasn't Mom mentioned her to me?"

"Mentioned what?" Mom startles us as she takes a seat at our table, plopping her purse on the floor next to her.

"We were just telling Madden about how Odette Hastings has really grown up," David replies.

Mom snorts. "She's not worth your time, Madden. Don't get me wrong, I adore Mrs. Hastings, but their family has no money and no connections."

"Why does that matter? At this point, if you *don't* approve, I might actually like her." Me and my brothers snicker. We've all been on the receiving end of Mom's unsuccessful setups.

Mom leans in to make sure no one will overhear. "Well, I'm just trying to help. You need to announce your campaign in a few months, and you're not making any headway on finding a wife who will advance your career. If you'd just let me–"

"Mom, let me figure this out on my own. The last thing I need is you marrying me off to some debutante." I shake my head in frustration.

"*Fine*. You let your father help, but you won't give me an inch. Alright. I won't bring it up again." She pouts.

"Mom, can't you at least give him Odette's number? What harm could it do?" David asks.

She sets her shoulders back and smiles smugly. "No need. We invited the Hastings to Thanksgiving next week. And when you see that Odette is no different from the other girls your father threw at you, you'll wish you'd had my help."

⊷

Windell family group chat:

Sophie: Happy Thanksgiving, family! I wish Sam and I could be there! We miss you all!

Madden: Miss you, Soph! Happy Turkey Day! *GIF of dancing turkey*

Sophie: BTW How's the wife hunt going?

Madden: Brooks, is it impossible for you to keep your mouth shut?

Madden: Also, it's excruciating. I've been on so many miserable dates.

Brooks: Don't worry, bro. Odette will knock your socks off today.

David: Let's hope so. I'm worried we'll need to cancel this entire campaign.

Dad: He's too picky. *eye roll emoji*

Mom: He won't let me set him up with the best girls in the Midwest, so I can't imagine what he'd see in the Hastings girl.

Sophie: You guys! I'm missing all the fun!

Sophie: Madden, I thought Odette was always such a sweetheart! You be nice to her!

Madden: You are all dead to me.

⊷

Walking into the kitchen at my Mom and Dad's house, I hear the muffled sounds of my parents bickering. My shoulders tense and I cringe. Their arguments are the soundtrack of my childhood, though holidays were usually the exception. Being a highly sought-after surgeon, Dad worked most holidays. I'm surprised that he is off today.

Mom is so busy pounding bread dough angrily into the counter that she doesn't hear me enter. I clear my throat and they both look up at me.

"Hey. Happy Thanksgiving," I mutter awkwardly, putting my hands in my pockets. "Anything I can help with?"

"You can mash those potatoes over there." Mom motions to the large pot on the gas stove. She looks like an innocent little Donna Reed today in her floral dress, pearls, and apron. But I know there's a demanding woman with high expectations underneath that facade.

Dad straightens from a crouch by the oven–checking the turkey temperature, I assume–and I see that he's wearing an apron with bold, black letters that say, "Trust me. I'm a doctor." He gives me an annoyed look. "I should warn you that Mom invited Heidi and her family at the last second."

My shoulders slump. I remember my date with Heidi. She talked about her purse-sized Pomeranian and her Dad's business the entire time. "Aren't we already having the Hastings over and a few others? Will there be enough room for everyone?"

David and Brooks walk into the kitchen to join us. They look at me with shifty eyes, perhaps sensing the tension, and ask Mom if she needs help with food prep. My sister Sophie was always the one who helped Mom in the kitchen, but since she moved away a few years ago, my brothers and I have stepped up.

Dad stomps out of the room, calling tersely over his shoulder, "Your mother has extended the table as far as it can possibly go so we can accommodate everyone... Including Heidi's furball."

Mom looks up from her dough and shoots lasers with her eyes at Dad's retreating back. "Your father is being dramatic. Heidi is a very nice girl. I think you should give her another chance. You might even fall in love and want to stay married to her for *more* than two years."

I feel a bit confused. Heidi was Dad's set-up, wasn't she? When did Mom get on board? "Is Heidi one of those eligible ladies you wanted me to date?"

Mom purses her lips and goes back to pounding her dough. "Maybe."

Brooks stirs the pot of green beans next to me and whispers, "Would you be mad if I flirt with Odette tonight? She's smokin' hot."

I turn to give him a snarky retort, but David turns from where he's standing behind us and whops him in the back of the head. "You're not the one looking for a wife, you dope. If anyone flirts with her, it should be Madden."

After finishing up the potatoes, I transfer them to the porcelain dish Mom set out and take them to the dining room. When I spot my place setting on the table, though, my jaw clenches.

Mom has me seated right between Heidi and Odette.

This is my own personal hell. It's like she wants me to compare the two women. Does she really think that will make Heidi look better? Who knows what's cooking inside that mind of hers.

Dad walks into the dining room, taking in the seating arrangements and my apparent horror. He snorts. "Just make the best of it. I suppose she's trying to help, even if it is *completely* overbearing."

I let out a heavy sigh and look at my dad. Despite him not being around much when I was younger, he's still the most level-headed person I know. "I'll just keep my mouth full the entire time so I don't have to speak."

Dad gives me a sympathetic look as I set the plate of potatoes down in the center of the table. "In my head, I thought it was going to be much easier than it has been to find someone tolerable. Now I just feel stupid." I scrub my hands over my face.

"Son, I hate to tell you this, but relationships are never convenient. And even when someone gets married to a person they actually love, it doesn't mean that marriage will work." He winces at his own words. "Sometimes you just have to do what needs to be done. Don't overthink it."

Well, that didn't make me feel any better. Knowing my parents are miserable with each other never seems to get any easier. And the thought of marrying someone–anyone–only to become just as miserable as them sends a bolt of panic through me.

I only have a month left to find someone to marry me, so I might as well meet Odette. I can always feign sickness and leave early if she's crazy. I absolutely refuse to let my mother manipulate me into giving Heidi another chance, though. I'd rather kiss my political career goodbye before marrying someone who carries a dog around in their purse.

I'm distracted and deep in thought when I walk back into the kitchen. Brooks swings his arm around my shoulder and leans in. "Bro, if you're going to meet your future wife tonight, don't you wish you would have worn different clothes?"

"What's wrong with these?" I look down at my dark jeans, leather belt, and white button-up shirt tucked in neatly. I thought I looked pretty good. This *is* my go-to look, after all.

Brooks can barely contain his grin as he peruses my outfit. "Not to sound creepy, Madden, but we all know your tush is your best feature, and those jeans aren't doing you any favors." He snaps me in the butt with a dishtowel.

I pivot on my heel and put him in a headlock. He whines and I burst out laughing. Brooks may be younger and more spry than me, but I spend a good amount of time in the gym. I can still take him.

David hears the commotion and turns to us. "You are both such children. And just because Mom went upstairs to get ready, doesn't mean she won't be pissed at you for wrestling in her kitchen."

He has a point. We stand up straight and get back to work.

"Brooks is right, though," David adds with a smirk. "You should've worn different jeans.

Chapter 5

Odette

♥

I let out a nervous sigh as we pull up to the Windell driveway in College Hill. Their home is a gorgeous, craftsman-style Victorian with white paneling and a brick path leading up to the wrap-around porch. Some stained glass windows are even still present. I take it in with a sigh. D.C. was beautiful, of course, but College Hill is absolutely charming.

We step out of the car into the chilly November air, and I help my dad out of the back seat. Thankfully, the brick path is smooth enough for him to manage.

When Mom grabs his other arm, I take a moment to smooth down my grey sweater dress and brace myself for this evening. I'm relieved when I look down and see my black leggings aren't covered with lint. I even wore some cute booties and spent extra time on my hair. I'm not sure why I care so much. It's not like Madden and I are going to ride off into the sunset and live happily ever after. Especially since he didn't even remember me from high school, which I'm still mildly irritated about.

I manage to plaster a smile on my face as Mom rings the doorbell. Mrs. Windell answers exuberantly. "Welcome, welcome! We're so happy to have you!"

I remember Dr. and Mrs. Windell from my high school days, and I swear Mrs. Windell hasn't aged a bit. She's just as pretty and well-coiffed as I remember, with her petite stature and dark hair. I stand back as she helps my Dad bring his walker inside and embraces my Mom in a quick hug.

"Odette, we're so thrilled you could join us as well." Mrs. Windell turns to me with a bright smile, though it doesn't meet her eyes. Maybe she's just tired from preparing Thanksgiving dinner.

"Thank you so much for having us." I nod to her as I step inside. "Your home is so charming."

Charming is an understatement. Their home is large and grandiose, but also very inviting. It looks like they have updated and added on throughout the years, but the house has still kept its original charm. I can see two fireplaces from the entryway, their hearths lit and crackling, keeping the home warm and cozy. The smell of freshly baked bread and turkey makes my stomach growl hungrily.

Mrs. Windell leads us through the foyer and into the dining room, where four extremely tall, handsome men are chatting amiably with each other. The tallest of them I recognize as Dr. Windell. His hair has turned more grey than blonde since the last time I saw him, but he's still a very nice-looking man.

They stop their conversation when we enter. Dr. Windell steps forward with a warm smile, but before he can utter a word, the one with long, curly hair and dimples strides forward to take my hand.

"Enchanté, mademoiselle," he says with a wink and a quick kiss to the back of my captive hand.

"Don't mind Brooks. He can't seem to behave himself. He may look like an adult, but he has the maturity of a 6-year-old," Dr. Windell says seriously, though a smile plays at the corner of his lips.

My parents laugh politely. Brooks just shrugs and gives us a dimply grin as he steps back.

Mrs. Windell gestures to the men lined up in her dining room. "Odette, this is my husband, Ted." She briefly touches Dr. Windell's arm, who I cannot imagine referring to as simply *Ted*. "And you've now met my youngest son, Brooks." She shoots a quick glare in his direction. "I'm sure you remember my oldest, Madden?"

My mouth becomes dry, and the blood drains from my face as soon as I look at him. Has he somehow become better looking since I last saw him? I want to be unaffected by him and his stupid chiseled jaw, broad, muscled shoulders, and wavy, dark-blonde hair–the type I'd love to run my fingers through. But his handsomeness is incredibly distracting.

Pull yourself together, Odette! You're not some silly teenager who's never seen a handsome man before.

Madden's glacier-blue eyes are wide with shock. He probably realizes now that he saw me at the reunion and didn't know who I was. The thought gives me a little jolt of satisfaction.

"Wow. Hi, Odette... or, Red?" He smirks, then has the grace to look a little flustered. "I'm sorry for not recognizing you before. That was very rude of me."

He looks into my eyes and flashes his gorgeous, pearly white smile. I swear the room just got ten degrees hotter. It must be the fireplace.

Why does my skin have to be so pale? I'm sure the entire room just watched my face change color like a mood ring.

Pulling myself together, I try to speak evenly, but my voice comes out as more of a high-pitched squeak. "That's okay! Good to see you again." *Wow, Odette. That's the blandest thing you could've said.*

The doorbell rings and Mrs. Windell scurries off to answer it while Dr. Windell introduces David, who I remember being several years younger than me.

"I'm sorry that our daughter, Sophie, couldn't make it this year," Dr. Windell says. "I'm sure she would've loved to see you all. Her husband is deploying to Afghanistan soon, so they're spending as much time together as possible."

Mrs. Windell returns to the room with a woman named Heidi and her parents, who look about the same age as Dr. & Mrs. Windell, and a pleasant-looking man named Drew and his little girl. After introductions have been made all around, our attention turns back to the table.

"Well, dinner is ready! Let's have a seat and get started! We have a few more guests coming, but they won't arrive until after seven." Dr. Windell says with a flourish toward the perfectly set table.

We look around for our places, marked with lovely floral place cards embossed in gold calligraphy. I definitely want to keep mine. Maybe I can sneak it into my purse without looking like a huge dork.

Once I find my seat, I immediately break out in a nervous sweat when I notice that Madden is seated next to me. The very poised and glamorous Heidi sits on his other side. Maybe she's his girlfriend?

Dr. Windell says a quick prayer and we pass the food around as multiple conversations start up at once, but I'm too busy sneaking peeks at Madden to contribute. He's chatting animatedly with his brothers across the table.

I hear everyone talking and laughing around me, but all my senses are tuned to the man sitting next to me. There's something more to Madden than just his looks, I decide. He has a confident presence–just like his father–and his intelligent eyes seem to look straight into my soul.

I hear Madden clear his throat. "Would you like some potatoes, Odette? I made them myself."

"Yes, please, I love carbohydrates." *Oh my gosh, quit being weird.*

Madden just chuckles. "Then you'll be happy to hear that my mother baked five different pies for dessert." He pauses and takes a deep breath

Is he nervous? The thought makes the tips of my ears flush warm.

He shifts in his seat to meet my eyes. "So... I heard that you just moved back to Wichita from D.C. What kind of work did you do there?"

I have suddenly forgotten what on earth I did for work in D.C. Thankfully, I make a quick recovery. "Oh, yes, I moved back this summer. I worked as a legislative assistant and really enjoyed it, but it's great to be back near my parents."

"I'm pretty interested in politics myself," Madden responds with a smile that quickly disappears as Brooks and David snicker from across the table. Within a few seconds, though, Brooks suddenly stops laughing and shrieks, then glares in Madden's direction.

I noticed Dr. Windell clear his throat as both he and Mrs. Windell send all three men a harsh look from their opposite ends of the table. The brothers sit up straight and look a little abashed.

Once their parents dive back into conversation with their guests, David whispers, "Behave, or Mom won't let us have dessert."

Madden must have sent another kick under the table because Brooks flinches. I can't help but laugh. Seeing them mess around makes me wish I had brothers of my own to tease.

After taking a few more bites of turkey and mashed potatoes, I hear a small yipping sound from under the table. I look over at Madden in surprise and see him looking next to him at Heidi. She smiles and pulls her large handbag from under the table, setting it on her lap. A fluffy, distinctly canine face peeks out of the purse and begins yipping even louder.

"Oh, Pompom!" Heidi giggles and looks at Madden. "Would you like to pet her?"

"No, thank you." He scrunches up his nose at the fluffy little dog. Heidi looks very annoyed.

I clear my throat to break the tension between Madden and Heidi, finally mustering up the gumption to make conversation. "So,

Madden... what do you do for work these days?"

His eyes briefly shift to his brothers, almost as if he's warning them not to say a word. David and Brooks quickly stuff their faces full of food and look down as if the tablecloth has suddenly become extremely interesting. "I worked with Bennington and Associates law firm for a few years, but I just quit a few weeks ago to pursue other opportunities. How about you?"

I squirm uncomfortably in my chair. "Actually, I haven't found work yet since moving back. I've looked into a few jobs, but it's hard to find anything that would still allow me to help my parents during the day." I avoid his eyes. Here I am, unemployed, sitting next to a successful lawyer.

"Right, that makes sense." Madden changes the subject, thank goodness. "What are your interests, then? Do you have any hobbies?"

I relax a bit, far more comfortable with this topic. "I'm a bookworm, actually. All I need for entertainment is a book and a strong cup of coffee." I answer before taking another bite of mashed potatoes. The man certainly knows how to mash a potato. Must be those biceps I see flexing through his shirt every time he moves.

"Did you visit The Library of Congress when you lived in D.C.?"

I bring my eyes back up to meet his and hope he didn't notice me staring at his brawny arms. "It's by far my favorite place! I tried to make it over there as much as possible. You've been?"

"Yes! I stop by whenever I'm in town. It's the most beautiful library I've ever seen."

My stomach flutters with butterflies. I am a sucker for a man who appreciates a wonderful library.

Drew, seated on Heidi's other side, overhears our conversation and jumps in. "Did I hear you mention the Library of Congress? I haven't been yet, but it's on my bucket list." This is the first time I've heard him speak since he's been busy with his daughter all evening.

Madden chuckles. "Drew is from Seattle. He hasn't been to D.C. yet."

"Oh, how long have you lived in Kansas?" I lean forward to ask Drew, raising my voice slightly so he'll hear me over the other conversations around us.

Drew smiles. "Ten years now. I work in the OR with Dr. Windell, so I have little time to travel."

Heidi has moved her attention to Madden now that Drew and I are chatting. I watch her rest her long fingernails on his shoulder as she bats her eyelash extensions at him. An unknown heat spreads through me. I feel tingly, but not in a good way. More like a lioness protecting her territory, which is ridiculous since Madden isn't mine.

And I don't want him to be. Right?

✦

Madden

As I wash my hands in the bathroom, I take a deep breath and look in the mirror. I look like I've aged ten years during this one dinner. My skin is pale, I have bags under my eyes, and is that a pimple?! What am I, fourteen again?

Attempting to get to know Odette with Heidi and her dog here is brutal! I'm usually so charming with women–I mean, maybe not as much as Brooks, but I've had no issues getting a woman's attention before.

My shock at how much Odette has changed isn't helping matters, either. It would be much easier to have a levelheaded conversation if she was still gangly and frizzy-haired. But no, she had to grow up. Now I can't help but notice the light dusting of freckles across her skin, how her gangly limbs have turned into lean curves, and how she has clearly learned to smooth her unruly hair into silky auburn curls.

I can't believe I didn't recognize her at our reunion. No wonder she seemed annoyed and made up a fake name. As soon as I realized this evening that Odette was the woman from my reunion, all thoughts of faking sick to get out of here vanished.

I splash my face with cold water and rest my forearms on the bathroom vanity. *Come on, Madden! If you can get Odette alone for a moment, maybe she'll agree to go on a date with you. Alone. Without Heidi and her freaking dog.*

This is my chance to get her number. She's well educated, poised, gorgeous, and doesn't carry any pets in her purse. She could be perfect, and would definitely look striking on my campaign pamphlets.

When reality hits again, I wince. How can I ever convince her to fake-marry me? There's no way she would ever agree to that.

At this point, I'm running out of options. I have to try or give up my campaign. It's worth a shot, at least. I sigh.

I give myself a reassuring nod in the mirror and then head back out to the dining room. Thankfully, Paul Newhouse and his wife, Marie, have arrived just in time for dessert. I'm anxious to see how he reacts to Odette.

The dining room is packed now. I notice that my parents are on opposite sides of the large room. Coincidence? Probably not. I'm half-convinced that my parents only invite people over because they hate spending time alone together.

I make my way over to Odette, hoping to find a private moment to ask her out. But as I reach her side, I look up and see Paul and his wife walking toward us. His wife is tall, slim, and gray-haired just like he is. They stride over and glance curiously between Odette and I.

"Madden! Happy Thanksgiving. And who is this lovely young lady?" Paul looks at me with a raised eyebrow.

"Paul, this is Odette Hastings. We went to high school together and our mothers are good friends." I try to keep my facial expression neutral.

Paul's mouth slowly lifts into a grin. He introduces himself and his wife to Odette.

"It's really nice to meet you, Mr. and Mrs. Newhouse." Odette smiles and shakes their hands politely. "How do you know the Windells?"

Without skipping a beat, Paul exclaims, "Well, I have the honor of being Madden's campaign manager! Inspiring young man, this one." He claps me on the back with a genuine smile.

Odette looks surprised. "Campaign manager? What sort of campaign?"

Paul glances at me apologetically once he realizes that I hadn't informed Odette of my congressional aspirations yet.

I shift on my feet and run a hand through my hair. "I'm putting my hat in the race to become Kansas's state representative for the fourth district."

Odette stares at me with a stunned expression. "That's amazing! I had no idea. Well, as you know, I have experience in politics, so if you need any help with your campaign, I'd be happy to help!" She looks genuinely excited about the prospect, making my heart soar. I get lost in her twinkling green eyes as we grin at each other.

I'm pretty sure this woman fell straight from heaven and into this dining room. Seeing Odette's passion for politics and her excitement for me to run makes me way happier than I probably should be. But it's a wonderful contrast to my ex-fiancée's negativity about my aspirations.

"Oh, I have a feeling you could be a *great* help, Odette. Possibly just what Madden needs." Paul smirks at me, and Odette looks a little confused.

"Well, now that I've eaten my body weight in turkey and pie, my mom and I need to get Dad home. Madden, it was nice seeing you again, and Paul, it was lovely to meet you!"

"Let me walk you out," I say. This might be my last chance.

Everyone says their goodbyes to the Hastings and then we walk out into the frigid November night. Odette and I amble slowly behind her parents, side by side. Once her parents reach their car, Mrs. Hastings helps her husband with his walker.

It's now or never.

Odette looks up at me, shifting on her feet. "It was nice seeing you."

"You as well." I smile. "Actually, I was wondering... could I see you again?"

Her cheeks turn bright red. "Sure. I'd like that."

I pull my phone out of my pocket. "What's your phone number? I'll text you and we can set up a date."

Odette punches her number into my phone, turning more red by the second, and then bids me a bashful farewell before ducking into her parents' car.

After the Hastings drive away, I walk back inside and do my best to ignore Paul when he turns to me with gleaming eyes and a knowing grin on his face.

≈

Once I'm back at my apartment that evening, I have time to process my thoughts. I felt discouraged after six months of failed dates, but after spending the evening in Odette's presence, it suddenly doesn't seem so impossible anymore. It's easy to envision us together. Not only could she help me get to Congress, but I think I'd actually enjoy being around her. And we'd only need to stay married for a few years, anyway. This could work.

Now I just have to convince her that this "marriage of convenience" *isn't* a completely boneheaded idea. What could I give her to make it worth her while? Judging by their vehicle, it seems like my mother was right: they don't have much money. And she mentioned her father's therapies. Do they need help paying for those?

I groan, feeling like a jerk. Offering marriage to girls who just want their trust funds is one thing. But when I consider marrying Odette, I feel short of breath. What will she think of me for making such an offer?

Why does it feel so different with her?

Chapter 6

Odette

♥

I wake up the next morning with a smile on my face. Not only was Thanksgiving dinner delightful, but ever since Madden asked for my number, I can't stop smiling. I was certainly a bit annoyed with him at the reunion, but last night I thought I sensed a mutual attraction between us. I can't wait to explore that more on our date, whenever that happens.

It was more than Madden, though. Before yesterday, I never realized how quiet and somber our holidays were. I adore my parents and I've loved our simple celebrations, but there was something so fun about a home bursting with people and activity, siblings teasing each other, and friends stopping by. Being an only child, I haven't experienced anything like it. I felt welcomed and included, like I belonged there.

I roll over to check my phone and see that I have twelve missed texts from Kate. She made me promise to keep her updated, and I completely forgot to check my phone all last evening.

Kate: Happy Thanksgiving!

Kate: How are things at the Windells?

Kate: *GIF of bugs bunny checking his watch and tapping his foot*

Kate: Ok, send a knife emoji if you need me to come rescue you.

Kate: But if it's going well, send a kiss emoji.

Kate: Can you at least tell me what the table décor looks like? Diane has exquisite taste.

Kate: What are the perks of being the best friend if I don't get a play-by-play of your awkward, Thanksgiving blind-ish date?!

Kate: Ok, you're killing me, Odette.

Kate: OMG Are you and Madden making out in a closet?!

Kate: Did you run off to the courthouse for a quick marriage?

Kate: I can't believe you didn't invite me to the wedding.

Kate: I already have the perfect heart-patterned bridesmaid dress. Now I'll never have a chance to wear it.

I giggle and roll my eyes. Kate is off work today, so I decide to just call her.

She answers her phone in a grim tone. "Hello? Who is this?"

"Good morning to you, too, Kate."

"Oh, is this my long-lost best friend?"

"If you don't stop acting so dramatic, I won't breathe a word about our Thanksgiving at Ted and Diane's."

"*Oh my gosh,* you call them Ted and Diane now? So you and Madden really got hitched?"

"Hardy har har. I am still painfully single. But Madden *did* ask for my number."

"*What*? Why didn't you lead with that?"

I shrug, though Kate can't see it. "Dramatic effect."

"Well, cut the drama and tell me what happened!"

I flop back on my bed and smile to myself, remembering Madden's blue eyes looking into mine as he asked for my phone number. "Madden is so handsome that it's intimidating. I felt nervous talking to him, though watching him and his brothers tease each other like little boys was hilarious. It kind of made me wish I had siblings to heckle, you know? And then, right before we left, he caught my arm and asked for my number."

"That's amazing! Teenage Kate is so jealous right now. Though, just so you know, siblings aren't that great. My little brother always drove me nuts."

I chuckle. "Hey, did you know he's running for Congress?"

Her surprised gasp through the phone is loud in my ears. "I hadn't heard that! I could see him being an awesome Congressman. I bet a campaign is going to keep him awfully busy."

"Oh, yeah, you're right. Maybe he won't even have time to date." My face falls with the realization.

I hear muffled giggles in the background. "Ugh. I'm sorry to cut this short, but the twins just got up, so I have to go."

"Alright. Kiss those cuties for me!"

"Will do! Keep me posted on the Madden situation!"

We say goodbye, and then I sit up in my bed for a moment to consider what Kate said. It really does seem like terrible timing for Madden to start dating someone. I probably shouldn't get my hopes up.

⊰

The next week goes by uneventfully. I haven't heard a peep from Madden, and I can't help but feel disappointed. Going on a date with him would've been amazing.

Tonight, I'm at Home Depot with my parents, looking for an artificial Christmas tree. We've always gone to the tree farm and selected the perfect Fraser fir, but it would be too difficult for Dad to get around a tree farm this year.

We're standing in an aisle filled with inflatable yard ornaments, and my mother begs Dad to splurge on a fuzzy, grinning Christmas llama to spruce up their yard.

"It even dons a plaid scarf and plays music!" My mom reads off the box.

Dad looks at me and lets out an exasperated sigh, but agrees, so I heft the box into the cart for them. He acts annoyed, but I know he'd buy a million inflatable llamas if it would make Mom happy.

"Sweetie, it's been over a week now. Any word from... that boy? I'm sorry, I can't think of his name." Dad glances at me with a raised eyebrow.

I let out a heavy sigh that I just can't seem to suppress anymore. I've been trying all week to convince myself that I'm not disappointed. "It's Madden. And, no, I'm afraid not." I guess I can add one more name to the list of guys who thought I was boring.

Dad gives my hand a squeeze. "Well, that's surprising. I thought he was making eyes at you the entire evening."

I chuckle at Dad's choice of words. "I'm sure that Madden has plenty of other prospects. I probably didn't make much of an impression." I can never seem to make a good first impression. Madden couldn't even remember who I was.

"If he thinks he can find a smarter, prettier, or better woman than my Odette, then he's an imbecile. And you make pretty decent coffee, too."

I put a hand over my heart in feigned shock. "Well! I never thought I'd hear those words out of your mouth."

"I'm feeling generous today." He winks.

As usual, Dad puts a smile on my face. I pull him into a hug, cherishing the moment. Little things like this make me grateful that I moved back.

One artificial tree and one inflatable llama later, we return home to decorate. I had always flown home for holidays in years past, but it's been a while since I was here to decorate the tree with Mom and Dad.

We laugh together as we pull out the old ornaments and share our favorite Christmas memories. The house feels cozy and romantic with the twinkling lights on the tree, cinnamon-scented candles, and the little glass snow village my mom sets up every year. We transform their home into a little winter cottage.

Glancing outside, I notice that the sun is beginning to go down, so I throw on my coat and gloves and head outside to set up Mom's llama before it gets too dark.

Just as I'm getting the ridiculous Christmas llama inflated, I see the headlights of a black Audi pull into our driveway. Someone must've made a wrong turn.

But the car parks, to my surprise, and out steps Madden Windell in jeans and a black pea coat with a cocky grin on his face–dreamy as ever.

Seeing him takes me by surprise, so much so that I don't see the extension cord wrapped around my ankle. As I step toward him, the cord snags and I topple over onto the half-inflated llama. With a rush of embarrassment, I realize that I landed right between the llama's hind legs, putting us in a very compromising position.

A laugh bursts out of Madden, but he tries to compose himself as he runs over to help me up. My foot is still caught in the cord, though, and I stumble again, this time right into his strong arms. He grabs my waist to steady me, and our faces are only inches apart when I look up to thank him. I feel dizzy. Somehow, his face is even more handsome up close.

Coming back to our senses, we laugh awkwardly and he steps back to put an appropriate amount of space between us.

"I'm sorry for laughing. That was just such a sight. And is that a Christmas... llama?" Madden nudges the downed inflatable creature with his foot.

I pin him with an annoyed glare. "I assume you didn't come over here just to watch me assault an inflatable, did you?"

"No, of course not... Llama tell you how much I love whimsical Christmas décor." He smiles, looking very proud of himself for his pun, and I groan. "Actually, I really do think it's great. My mom never allowed fun decorations like this."

"Well, it's freezing out here now that the sun is down. Do you want to come inside?"

"Yeah, that would be great." He takes one last look at the llama, which is now fully Inflated and playing Christmas music just like the box said it would. Madden chuckles as he follows me through the front door.

My parents look surprised and delighted to see me walk through the door with Madden. Dad shoots me a quick wink and my face heats. I hope Madden doesn't notice.

"Madden Windell! To what do we owe the pleasure?" My mom beams up at him.

"I just stopped by to see Odette. I hope that's okay," he admits—a bit bashfully, I note with pleasure.

I take his coat for him and hang it on the coat rack, but not before I catch a quick whiff. Oh my, It smells even more heavenly than I imagined. I detect a hint of spice mixed with a scent that I can only assume is uniquely Madden. Not that I've ever imagined how he smells.

As I remove my own coat, I glance at my faded, black leggings and old college sweatshirt and wish I would've put a little more effort into my appearance this morning. Dad pushes Mom into the kitchen and announces, "We were just about to heat up some apple cider! Would you like some, Madden?"

I shake my head at how obvious my parents are behaving, but Madden responds politely. "Absolutely. I love cider."

We take our seats on the worn loveseat by the tree. Again, his proximity makes it hard for me to think clearly. At least the room is lit by the dim Christmas lights alone, so hopefully, he can't see how red my cheeks are. Stupid pale skin.

Madden looks totally cool and collected. I'm most likely too dorky to affect him in the same way he affects me. He drapes his arm across the back of the sofa. "I apologize for not calling or stopping by sooner. Paul—er—my campaign manager and myself had several urgent meetings this past week."

I surreptitiously lean forward to put some distance between us and try to fake nonchalance. "It *has* been a week already, hasn't it? Time sure flies during the holidays."

He eyes me quizzically–probably silently calling my bluff. "It sure does." One side of his mouth curves up into a smile. "I actually came by to ask you a question. It's going to seem a little odd, but I promise I'll explain another time."

"That's pretty vague, but I'll try to answer as best I can." I nervously twirl my ponytail and realize it's shifted off to the side. Just my luck. One more reason I should've looked in the mirror before sitting down.

"I guess I'll just jump right in." He clears his throat. "What I want to know is, what exactly are your political stances?"

I slump in confusion. Is this a job interview? That definitely wasn't the question I expected. Still, I *would* love to work on his campaign, to feel useful again. I consider for a moment and then respond. "I'm registered as a Libertarian."

Madden's eyebrows shoot up and I hurry on, worried that he'll write me off if I don't explain myself quickly. "I know you might think I'm odd for affiliating with a third party, but I just don't think either of the major parties adequately reflects what I believe are our most important American values: liberty and freedom. I want people to have as much autonomy over their land and rights as they possibly can. "

Madden's face lights up in a full smile, showing his perfectly straight teeth. "Actually, I agree with you. Politics have become so polarized over the years. It seems like politicians are more worried about their own paychecks than actually taking care of their constituents. I really want to change that. I'm hoping I can pave the way for more independent thinkers to run for office in the future."

His gaze lingers on mine for a few moments longer than what's probably appropriate for a job interview. I'm becoming more confused by the second, but I return his smile all the same. I'm relieved to hear that I could be a great fit to help on his campaign. "I hardly ever met like-minded individuals in D.C., so this conversation is incredibly refreshing."

Mom and Dad interrupt us to deliver two mugs of hot apple cider. We all enjoy polite conversation for a while and Madden compliments my Mom on her choice of yard decor. Once our mugs are empty, Madden announces that he needs to head home.

"Thank you for answering my question," he says in a low voice as I walk him to the door. "You've given me exactly what I needed."

"Glad I could help!" I'm still confused, though. Did he ask for my number at Thanksgiving because he liked me as a person or just as a potential employee? I shake the thought away as I hand him his coat.

"Odette, would you mind if we met up for our date on Tuesday? I have something I'd love to show you. Paul and I need to iron out a few details first." His eyes shift to the floor.

And now I'm even more confused. If it's a date, what does his campaign manager have to do with it? "Sure, that sounds great. I look forward to it."

I watch him from the doorway as he drives away, wondering why on earth he came over just to talk to me about politics. There's something strange about all of this.

Chapter 7

Madden

♥

A few days after my visit to Odette, I wait for her outside the Wichita Historical Museum. Only folks from Wichita would care to come to this museum, as it's not a big tourist destination–though nothing in Wichita is. If I have any chance of getting her on board with this outlandish idea, I need to explain some of my family history first.

The museum is located downtown in a small brick building. There's a great café next door, where I hope Odette will agree to have lunch with me afterward, but I'm doubtful. After expressing my intentions, she might just slap me in the face and run away.

My palms are sweaty, and I have dark circles under my eyes from lack of sleep. I knew this whole campaign would be grueling, but I had no clue what an emotional minefield actually lay ahead of me. The pressure of being in the public eye along with trying to find some political arm candy has already been completely exasperating.

Kansas is having one of its random warm days in December, but I'm not complaining; I'll accept any break from coats and scarves that I can get. I'm comfortable in my jeans and long-sleeved Henley. It may be 20 degrees and snowy tomorrow, though. Who knows with the Midwest.

I turn my head when I hear a vehicle rumbling a little too loudly nearby, and I'm surprised to see Odette driving up in a rickety old

Buick. She parks near the museum and climbs out of the rusty car, slamming the door with a loud creaking sound.

Taking in her angelic face as she steps onto the sidewalk, the wind whipping her lovely hair around her, I've all but forgotten the old Buick. She's dressed in dark jeans and a white sweater, but I think I liked her even better the other day in her leggings and baggy sweatshirt. She seemed so relaxed at her parent's house, with no makeup and a pair of Harry-Potter-style glasses on her nose. I don't think I've ever been attracted to Harry Potter glasses before, but she somehow made them look sexy. She's not wearing her glasses today, though. She must have contacts.

Her smile makes me feel a little less nervous. "Good morning. You look lovely," I say, making her blush.

We enter the building and she looks around curiously, grabbing a pamphlet from the front counter as we stride by. "I can't believe I lived in Wichita for eighteen years but have never been here before!"

Chuckling, I put my hand on her shoulder, but when I feel her tense up nervously, I quickly bring my hand back to my side. I love how shy she is, but I don't want to make her uncomfortable. When we walk to the first exhibit, she stops and reads the plaque, which explains how the *Keeper of the Plains* ended up in Wichita.

"As much as I love reading about Wichita's history, I'm terribly curious why you wanted to meet here today. Is this where you usually bring your dates?" She raises her eyebrows.

I chuckle nervously. "No. I've never brought a date here before. Actually, I wanted to show you a piece of my family history. My great, great grandparents are one of my inspirations to run for Congress."

She looks up from the exhibit and gives me an endearing look. "That's very sweet. I'm sure your devotion to family is just one more thing that will make you stand out when you run for Congress."

I cringe at her choice of words. If only she knew how important *devotion to family* really is to voters.

We continue making our way through the museum. I can't help but notice with a grin that Odette stops to read the plaques at each exhibit. There are two types of people who go to museums: those who read every word and those who fly through the entire building so they can leave sooner. Odette is clearly a reader. I appreciate that; I'm the same way.

Finally, after almost an hour of touring the little museum, we arrive at the exhibit I wanted to show her. On the wall, there's an enlarged black-and-white photograph of my great-great-grandparents standing in front of a classic Victorian-craftsman home. I study Odette's face and wait to see if she notices.

"Wait. Is that your parents' house?" She looks at me with her eyebrows raised.

I can't help but smile at her surprised expression. "Yes, it is. Well, technically it was my great-great-grandparents' house first. They're the ones who originally built it." I pause and take a deep breath. "Adalbert and Clara were immigrants from Sweden. They met on the train from New York to Wichita. Adalbert was able to finish his education and then got a job at a bank, and Clara found work as a maid. Once they were married, they saved up so they could build the house. Their home is part of our family's heritage, and growing up hearing stories about them is a big part of my desire to be a Congressman."

Odette studies the photograph in amazement. "That's really incredible. What a wonderful family legacy."

I nod toward the display case below the photograph. "And that leather book is one of the many journals Grandpa Adalbert kept. He had them all published a few years before he died."

She looks at the old, decrepit journal and furrows her brow. "Have you read them all?"

I look away for a second, trying to hide my emotion, but my voice comes out thicker than I want it to. "I have. They were sometimes... devastating to read. My great-great-grandparents struggled to adjust when they first arrived in the U.S. There were so many immigrants arriving from Sweden daily, which didn't endear locals to them. They were often treated poorly, mocked for their accents and their different customs." I swallow my emotion and try to lighten my tone. "The last twenty years of their lives were happy, though. He wrote a lot about how much he loved his wife."

"Thank you for sharing this with me. I can see why you are so passionate about helping immigrants." She gently puts her hand on my shoulder in a comforting gesture. Clearly startled by her own boldness, though, she removes her hand quickly and twirls a lock of her hair around her finger. She twirled her hair the other night at her house, too. I wonder if she does that when she's nervous.

I turn back to the display "The U.S. actually made it pretty simple back then to become a citizen, even if the public didn't. We scaled back on approving citizenship after World War I, though. Immigration nowadays has become a grueling process. One of my primary goals in Congress will be to work towards getting the United States to grant citizenship to more people. I want to introduce a bill that will help streamline the process." I'm really hoping that telling Odette *why* I want to become a Congressman–why it's so important to me–will make her empathetic to my cause.

"You're a good man, Madden," Odette whispers, her eyes meeting mine.

Time stops. I could look into this woman's green eyes all day. But I have to ruin the moment. I have to announce my campaign next month, and I still need a wife to help my chances of winning this election. It's now or never.

I rub my sweaty palms down the front of my jeans. "So... there's actually something I need to talk to you about. It's going to sound completely insane, so I don't want you to answer right away. Take some time to think about it first. But not too much time because, well, I need to announce my campaign next month..." I trail off, feeling hopelessly stupid.

She takes a step back and I watch her defenses go up. She twirls her hair again. "Okay. What is it?"

I swallow nervously. "You said you wanted to help my campaign—and I *do* need your help—but I can't continue without... This is going to sound insane, I know, but I have no chance of success if I'm not...well, if I'm not married."

A bead of sweat drips down my brow as I watch her eyes almost bug out of her head. I wipe the sweat with the back of my hand and continue. "My campaign manager has studied exit polls and the statistics of past candidates. According to his research, I need to be a committed family man for voters to take me seriously."

She blinks a few times and then her cheeks flame with color. "You're not about to ask what I think you are, right?"

"I think we'd make a great team, Odette. If you'd marry me—specifically, within the next week or two—I believe we could both benefit from it. I can take care of you and your parents. My family has the means to set up the best care for your father, or anything else you need. Our political goals coincide. We could make a united front and change this country for the better, together," I say, my eyes pleading with her to agree.

She guffaws and looks around the room dramatically. "I'm sorry, is this museum actually a time machine? Have I somehow been transported back to the Dark Ages?" She grinds her jaw, her laughter turning to outrage.

I reach toward her, but she steps back and clenches her fists at her sides. I hold my hands up in front of me. "Listen, I was shocked at first, too. But we would be allies, working to make this country better. And it wouldn't have to be forever. Maybe just a year or two, depending on how the election goes."

Her jaw drops. "Do you honestly think I'm desperate enough to accept a temporary, loveless marriage just so you can add Congressman to your resume?"

"I'm not saying that–"

"And what makes you think we want your *financial assistance,* anyway? Do you have a problem with the way I'm caring for my father?"

I flinch. I hadn't considered how that part might sound to her. "No, of course not. I didn't mean–"

"You don't know anything about my dad's current care, and even if you did, it's none of your business."

I put my hands up in an effort to stop her as she turns and looks for the museum exit. "Okay, I'm sorry. I don't think I'm explaining this clearly." I scrub my hands down my face. When Paul had talked about it, it made a lot more sense. What did he say, again? I blurt, "People always marry for love nowadays, and over 50% of those marriages end in divorce!"

She halts and whirls to face me. "Oh! So you're saying I should just marry you because I'll never have a *real* happy marriage?"

"No!" This is officially worse than I imagined. "I'm making a mess of this. Please wait and I can–"

"No, I think you've been perfectly clear." She stomps toward the exit, throws the door open, and leaves without so much as glancing back at me.

I let her go, confident that nothing I say at this point will rescue me from the hole I just dug myself into. Maybe she needs some time to think like I did? Or maybe I'm just horrible with words and insulted her so terribly that she'll never speak to me again.

I groan and scuff the floor with the tip of my shoe. I only did this to save my campaign, but the thought of Odette never speaking to me again leaves an ache in my chest.

Chapter 8

Odette

♥

A few days after the random offer of marriage from *he who shall not be named*, I'm home alone. My parents went out to get some last-minute Christmas gifts for me and insisted that I stay home. I rarely have the house to myself, so I'm soaking up the quiet by reading a book by the Christmas tree.

Despite my best efforts, though, I'm distracted and frustrated. Madden's proposal was *so* out of line and insane. I couldn't even tell my parents about it because I was too embarrassed. I wish I could just forget the entire thing.

As I turn the page in my book, skimming the lines without actually reading anything, my phone lights up. I glance at the screen and see my Mom calling. She probably wants to know what size of sweater to get me.

"Hey, Mom!" I answer cheerfully

"Sweetheart." Her voice is shaky. "I need you to come to the hospital. It's your dad."

My heart stops inside my chest. "What happened? Is he okay?"

"He's going to be okay, but he fell pretty hard. I'll explain when you get here."

"I'm on my way."Grabbing the keys to the Buick, I rush to the hospital. Once I park and run to the emergency room, the nurse behind the counter directs me to my dad's room. I burst in–chest heaving, dreading the worst–but the room is calm. My mom is seated on a small armchair by the hospital bed, stroking my dad's hand as he sleeps comfortably under the thin blankets. They probably gave him something for the pain.

"I got here as fast as I could." I pant.

She crosses the room and wraps me in a tight embrace. "They'll take him back for x-rays soon." She walks back to Dad's side and gently caresses his face.

"Tell me what happened." I grab a chair from the wall and drag it next to hers.

"We went to Target to do some Christmas shopping, but when I was helping your Dad back into the car, he slipped and fell pretty hard onto the asphalt. The doctor thinks he fractured his hip." Her voice cracks on her last word.

Tears stream down my cheeks. "If I had been there to help, this never would have happened."

"This isn't anybody's fault. You can't be with us every second of every day, and we would never ask that of you. Don't beat yourself up." Mom hands me a tissue from the bedside table.

Over the next several hours, they confirm that my Dad's hip is broken and take him back for surgery. It takes several excruciating hours until, finally; the nurses roll him back into the room. He's groggy, but it's a relief to see him with his eyes open, awake and alert.

The doctor strides into the room then. He's a familiar-looking man with a surgical cap, hazel eyes, and broad shoulders, followed by an older woman with a sleek, bobbed haircut, wearing a brown sweater along with dress pants and loafers. She reminds me of the super-suit designer from *The Incredibles*.

The doctor's mouth pulls up in a smile on one side, and that's when I recognize him as Dr. Windell's coworker, Drew.

He shakes my Mom's hand with a gentle smile. "Sorry it took us so long to make our way over here. I was with another patient."

Dad speaks up in a hoarse, tired voice. "That's okay. I had these beautiful ladies to keep me company." At least his sense of humor is still intact.

"Very true." He smiles. "I'm Dr. Reed, and I performed your husband's surgery. We met on Thanksgiving."

"Oh, yes! I knew you looked terribly familiar. It's nice to see you again, although I wish it were under better circumstances." She musters up a smile, even though she must be exhausted.

"Mrs. Hastings, your husband already looks much better than he did even a few hours ago. The surgery went extremely well. We placed rods in his upper femur to secure the hip and didn't experience any hiccups. We will keep him here for a few nights to monitor."

"So happy to hear that, thank you for taking good care of my husband." Mom's voice is thick with emotion.

"Of course. I'm glad that I was the one on-call today." Drew gestures to the woman behind him. "Let me introduce you to Mrs. Neal. The hospital has assigned her to be your case manager. I'll be back in the morning to check-in, unless you have questions for me?"

"No questions right now. We'll see you in the morning," Dad croaks as he gives Mom's hand a squeeze.

Once Drew leaves, Mrs. Neal takes a step forward. She's a stern-looking woman. "As Dr. Reed mentioned, I'm Mrs. Neal, and I've been assigned as your case manager. I'm here to discuss future care." She pauses as she hands a packet of brochures to my parents. "It's our professional opinion that you set up round-the-clock care from this point forward. Mr. Hastings, since you're 75 and have several health concerns needing to be monitored, we recommend an in-home nurse or assisted living. Occupational therapy will also be required for your hip."

Tears fill my Mom's eyes. "Assisted living? Surely there are other options."

Mrs. Neal gives my Mom an empathetic smile, lightening her face considerably. "The decision is up to you and your family, of course. I know this isn't what anyone wants to hear, but we want to make sure that you're taken care of. The brochures I gave you should help you with the decision."

She pauses for a moment. "Another thing I'd like to suggest is giving your child, or perhaps a close friend, power of attorney for you both. Someone who can help make medical and financial decisions if the need arises. Here's my card with all of my contact information. Please don't hesitate to call with any questions." She leans forward and gives Mom her business card.

Once she leaves the room, my mom finally breaks down, releasing the tears she has probably been holding back all day. I rush to her side and wrap my arms around her. Something my Dad taught me years ago is that sometimes in life, there are no words to say and no fixing to be done. In those moments, it's okay to just be there for someone in silence. So that's what I do. I simply hold her until she calms down.

Once she's calm, she looks up at me with desperation in her eyes. "I don't know what we're going to do, Odette."

I grab a pad of paper and pen out of my purse. "Okay, let's hash this out. What do you guys have in savings? I mean, if you're comfortable talking about this with me."

"Of course, sweetie." Mom massages her temples. "We've almost completely depleted our retirement savings between the bills from your dad's stroke and having to repair the sewer line in the house last winter."

My mind is reeling. How can their savings be gone? I know when Dad sold his book store the profit was much less than they'd hoped for, but I had no idea things were this bad. I take a deep, steadying breath. "What about Social Security? You guys get that, right?"

Dad shakes his head from the hospital bed. "I was self-employed, so we only get a thousand dollars a month. Knowing what I know now, I would've paid more into Social Security to set us up better for retirement." He lets out a heavy sigh. "But when you're young, you don't really think about those things."

I blink a few times, trying to mask my deepening concern.

Mom bursts into tears all over again. "Our financial situation has weighed so heavily on me this past year. We didn't want to burden you with the details, but I suppose we really do need help figuring this out. Would you be willing to be our power of attorney?"

"Of course." I put my hand on her shoulder, blinking back tears. "I moved back to help, after all. Why don't you let me take over the finances completely, so you can just focus on Dad?"

She puts her hand on top of mine. "We can't thank you enough."

"I'm sorry I wasn't more careful." Dad hangs his head. "I feel like I have been nothing but a burden to you both in the past year."

Mom moves to his bedside and brings her hand up to cradle his face in her palm. "You stop that kind of talk. It has been my greatest joy to care for you all these years. In sickness and in health, remember?"

A lump forms in my throat. "You just focus on getting better, Dad. I'll figure something out."

⊰⊱

At one o'clock in the morning, I arrive back home by myself. There was nothing I could do to convince Mom to come home with me. She wouldn't leave Dad's side. Maybe she'll miraculously get some sleep on the uncomfortable pull-out bed in the hospital room, but I doubt it.

I take a quick shower and put on my comfiest pajamas. Despite my complete exhaustion after today's events, though, sleep doesn't come.

Finally, I give up and pad back out to the living room to find something to clean. When I enter the main part of the house, my eyes land on the only item out of place: my purse. I threw it on the table when I arrived home, causing the brochures from the case manager to spill out. Grabbing my laptop from the kitchen counter, I sit down at the table, open the brochures, and begin my research.

After hours of pouring over the brochures, Googling links on my MacBook, and guzzling copious amounts of coffee, I've finally written our three best options down:

One: See if the bank will give us a loan to update the house and make it safe for Dad.

He'll need a wheelchair ramp to replace the stairs out front, a handicap-accessible shower, and rails in the bathrooms and hallway. And those are just the beginning of the corrections we would need. I consider what Mom told me about their finances today and breathe a heavy sigh. The bank will almost certainly reject their loan application. Rubbing my eyes, I look down at the second option.

Two: Sell the house and move my parents into an assisted living home.

I sigh again. This one seems just as unlikely as the first. The good places are expensive, and since my parents' house isn't paid off, they would hardly make enough money from the sale to settle their existing debts.

In a fit of exasperation around 5:00 AM, I jotted down the third option: go with option two, but sell a kidney and get a full-time job to afford the best place for my parents.

I blow a strand of hair out of my eyes. It would have to be a pretty good job to pay enough for assisted living *and* all of my own expenses. Where would I live? Another obvious downside is that I wouldn't get to spend much time with my parents–and I would be short a kidney.

There's a fourth option that I refuse to include in my notes, but it's still there in the back of my head. It would solve all of these problems instantly.

Marry Madden Windell.

He said he has the means to take care of me and my parents–and judging by his car and his parents' home in College Hill; I believe it. And he *did* say that we could go our separate ways after a few years. A mutually beneficial arrangement doesn't look so bad now. Taking care of my parents is more important to me than anything.

More important than my pride? My freedom?

I stand up and stretch my arms over my head. The sky outside shows the first signs of morning, a twinge of light turning the blackness dark blue. I've been up all night and need some sleep. With a heavy sigh, I head back to my bedroom.

I'll decide what to do about this in the morning.

Chapter 9

Madden

♥

Last night, my parents found out about Mr. Hastings' surgery from the prayer chain at their church. Ever since my dad called to tell me about it, I've wracked my brain trying to decide what to do. I want to reach out to Odette, but I'm pretty sure she still hates me. I also thought about delivering some food to their house, but I don't know if anyone would be home to receive it. And I definitely don't want Odette to think I'm just being nice to entice her to marry me.

Finally, I decide to take a card and some get-well-soon balloons to the hospital. It just doesn't sit right with me to ignore the situation completely.

I walk into the hospital looking like a doofus, I'm sure, with my bouquet of colorful balloons. The store even had a llama balloon, and I'm pretty sure that the Hastings like llamas, so I grabbed that one, too. It's still fairly early in the morning. I hope to sneak in and out quickly before Odette arrives.

I have to admit that a part of me will be disappointed if I don't get to see her, though. I feel oddly drawn to her, like a mosquito to bright light. Well, maybe that's a terrible example. That's how mosquitoes get zapped. I should never say that to Odette.

The nurses at the front counter recognize me right away, since my dad has been a surgeon on this floor for decades. Non-family visitors aren't allowed before 9:00 AM, but they say nothing when I ask for Mr. Hastings' room number.

I walk into the room to find Odette's parents awake and eating breakfast together. Their faces light up when they see me.

"Madden! What a surprise!" Mrs. Hastings gets up from the little armchair by the bed to greet me. She and her husband both have dark circles under their eyes. I should've brought coffee instead of balloons.

"I just wanted to bring a little something to cheer you up. I hope you heal quickly, Mr. Hastings." I nod to Mr. Hastings in the hospital bed as I hand Mrs. Hastings the balloon bouquet.

Mrs. Hastings' face lights up in excitement. "Well, aren't you just the sweetest thing! Goodness, is this a llama balloon?!"

"I couldn't resist." If only I could get on Odette's good side so easily. Then again, I didn't ask her Mom to marry me in exchange for money.

"Well, thank you! It's adorable. We're so happy that you stopped by. I'm terribly sorry Odette's not here yet. It's unlike her to sleep so late, but I bet she didn't sleep much last night." A shadow of exhaustion passes over Mrs. Hastings' face.

"That's okay. I just wanted to stop in real quick, but please let me know if you need anything. Or, if you get tired of cafeteria food, I can be your own personal GrubHub driver." I gesture toward their breakfast trays.

"Very thoughtful of you. I might take you up on that offer." Mr. Hastings winks and his wife chuckles.

"I'll let you two get back to your breakfast. I wrote my number on the back of the llama balloon if you need anything."

We say our goodbyes and I exit the room, quickly making my way past the front desk while I try to ignore the pit of disappointment in my stomach. I didn't get to see Odette.

I'm so enamored with my own thoughts that I don't even notice her coming towards me down the hall. She must not have noticed me, either, because we collide, the force almost knocking her over.

"Ope! I'm so sorry!" I gently grab her arms to steady her.

"Madden!" She looks surprised to see me, and a blush creeps into her cheeks. "Sorry, I was looking at my phone and didn't even see you."

I stare into her eyes for a few seconds too long, trying to figure out what to say next. I clear my throat. "I heard about your dad's surgery and I wanted to stop in and check on him."

"Oh, thank you. That was nice." She says with a somber expression. "I'm glad I ran into you, actually. I was going to call you later. Do you think we could get together and talk, maybe later this evening?"

My heart quickens. "I'd love that. I could bring over some dinner."

"Yes, that sounds good. Would seven o'clock at my parent's place work for you?" She bites her bottom lip nervously.

I nod in agreement, and then she ducks past me into her dad's room without another word. I stare after her for a moment–shock written all over my face, I'm sure–and then remember where I am, but not before the nurse at the front desk notices and looks at me with one eyebrow raised. After leaving the hospital, I drive to a local coffee shop for my meeting with Paul. I walk inside and give my order to the barista. I'm a simple black coffee kind of man, and it doesn't take long to get my freshly brewed mug.

Taking a seat across from Paul, I notice he already has three empty mugs on the table next to him. Obviously, he's been here for a while. "Good to see you, Paul."

"Good morning. We need to decide what to do with your campaign." He anxiously scrubs both hands down his face. "Have you talked to Odette?"

"Well, you know how terribly things went at the museum last week." I rub the back of my neck. "But I actually saw her just now at the hospital. She wants to get together this evening."

"Really? Maybe she's changed her mind." Paul picks up a mug and takes a sip, then apparently remembers that it's empty and frowns.

"She certainly didn't seem angry, which is a step in the right direction. She wants to have dinner tonight. To talk." One side of my mouth curves up into a half-smile. I don't want to get my hopes up, but I think it's too late for that.

Paul's eyebrows raise in surprise. "Maybe she has come around to the idea after all? Although I have no idea why she would after you botched things up so badly at the museum."

"Thanks for the supportive words. How *does* one successfully propose a marriage of convenience?" I take a gulp of my coffee.

"I mean, you could have brought flowers or diamonds, but maybe that's just me." Paul shrugs.

"This isn't a normal marriage, Paul. Also, Odette doesn't seem like a flower and diamonds kind of girl. I think she'd be more impressed if I gave her a library."

"Then give her the deed to a library and seal the deal." Paul laughs.

"I'll try to be more suave tonight."

"*That's* the future Congressman I know." He gives me a quick punch to the shoulder, and I roll my eyes.

⤳

I spend the rest of the day preparing for tonight. Paul was right. I need to make this marriage look more enticing. I should show her what it would be like to be married to me, even for just a few years. Odette doesn't really know me, though, and I don't want to overdo it.

I order two meals, two desserts, and a bottle of wine from George's French Bistro. Then I head to a local flower shop and get a dozen yellow roses. Red seemed too romantic. Lastly, I pick up a leather-bound copy of Pride & Prejudice because I know she loves books. My sister, Sophie, made me read this years ago.

At a quarter to seven, I drive over to the Hastings' house feeling sweaty and nervous. Juggling the bags from George's and also the flower arrangement, I lean forward to ring the doorbell with my elbow. My stomach is a bundle of nerves as I wait in the frosty December air. When Odette finally opens the door, her eyes fly to all the packages in my arms. She reaches for a bag to help out and then leads me into the kitchen so I can set down the rest of the goods.

"What on earth, Madden? I thought you would just grab some burgers for dinner." She furrows her brow as she unpacks the food.

"Burgers? George's is so much better."

"Why the flowers?" She gives me a skeptical look, then buries her face in the petals and savors the scent of the roses.

"Well, our first date ended up pretty terrible, so I'm trying to do better tonight."

Her cheeks turn pink. "Why would you assume this is a date?"

"You asked me to come to your house at seven o'clock, Odette. This is either a date or a booty call." I raise my eyebrows up and down at her.

"Madden Windell, how dare you even suggest such a thing!" Her mouth gapes open for a moment, but once she takes in the smirk on my face, she relaxes her shoulders. Although her face looks very unamused.

"Sorry. I was attempting to lighten the mood." I grimace. "In all seriousness, I owe you an apology. I was brash and presumptive. I should have spent more time with you before bringing up the issue with my campaign. I'm surprised you even wanted to speak to me tonight at all."

"Thank you for apologizing. I *was* angry about your offer." Odette looks at her feet awkwardly. Her skin is more pale than usual and her hands begin to shake. "But things have changed. Which is why I asked you here tonight."

Taking a few steps, I stop in front of her. I want to take her hands in mine, but that would probably make her uncomfortable. I stifle the urge. "What is it?"

"Sorry. I'm nervous." She inhales deeply through her nose, then looks up at me. "I've been thinking about your proposal, and I believe I've changed my mind. About marrying you. If the offer still stands."

My heart begins beating so fast that it feels like it might fly out of my chest. I try to contain the huge grin threatening my face, but it's too late. "I was hoping you'd say that. But why the sudden change of heart?"

Her eyes brim with unshed tears. "It's my dad. I need you to know upfront." She pauses and searches for the right words. "He needs round-the-clock care. I've poured over our options and assisted living seems like the best choice, but... it's expensive." She twirls her hair nervously.

A tumult of emotion assaults my chest. I feel humbled that Odette is turning to me for help, but then shame burns through me at the thought. She's only turning to me because I offered her money in exchange for marriage. But this isn't Heidi or any of the other trust fund girls I dated. This is a desperate woman doing the only thing she can think of to save her parents.

And it was my idea. What kind of man takes advantage of a woman this way?

I swallow. "I'm sorry. That has to be a really tough decision. You know I'm willing to help however I can. We can find the best assisted living money can offer."

"You need a wife and I need money." She gives me a sad smile. "Why not help each other?"

Another bolt of shame. "I... thank you."

We stand there for a moment, unsure of what to say. What *do* you say when you agree to marry a virtual stranger for mercenary reasons?

Well, I suppose there's only one place to start.

"There are obviously a lot of details we need to hash out, but before that..." I slowly get down on one knee. "I'm really grateful that you changed your mind. Odette Martha Hastings, will you marry me?" I see a twinge of panic flash through her eyes. Hoping to put her at ease, I try one more joke. "I promise to buy you as many inflatable yard ornaments as your heart desires."

She laughs once, startled and perhaps a bit relieved. "Yes. But, please, don't buy me any inflatable yard decorations." She reaches to help me up. "And for the record, my middle name isn't Martha."

"What *is* your middle name?"

"Lynn."

When I stand back up, I'm mere inches from her, close enough that I can smell the scent of her shampoo. She smells delicious, like a tropical paradise.

Suddenly, I have an overwhelming desire to kiss her. She'd probably slap me if I did. This is uncharted territory. We're officially engaged, but if it's fake, do we still seal it with a kiss? I look from her lips to her eyes and swear I catch her studying my mouth, too. Maybe she wouldn't slap me after all.

Before I can stop myself, I slowly lean forward. I think she's leaning as well, but it's such a slight movement that I can't be sure. Is my mind simply playing tricks on me? My body hums with anticipation.

And then my phone rings loudly.

We jump apart like teenagers who've been caught by their parents. I'm sure my face is beet red. What was I thinking?

I pull my iPhone out of my back pocket to see who's calling. *Possibly Spam*, the screen flashes. A hoarse laugh escapes her lips. "You can answer it if you need to."

"It's just spam." I pocket my phone again. "Shall we eat?"

She nods and I pull her chair out for her, then take a seat across the table. We sit in awkward silence for several minutes, eating our meal. I'm not sure what to say. I proposed to her in exchange for money; she said yes, and then I almost kissed her. My mortification runs deep.

Odette finally breaks the silence. "So, I'll probably need a ring, huh?" She wrinkles her nose. "We can just get those silicone ones and call it good."

"No, I'm going to get you a nice ring, and please don't feel weird about it." I hesitate. This next part is awkward. "If I'm elected into Congress, people will notice you and what you're wearing. Plus, I don't want to look like a cheapskate."

"Oh. Right." She draws in a deep breath and blows out the air dramatically. "I hope I can be convincing. I'm a terrible actress. What exactly do you need me to do?"

"Nothing yet." I fold my hands in front of me on the table. "For now, it might be smart to write down some of our terms. For the marriage, I mean. Then we'll be more prepared when we meet with my lawyer to sign paperwork."

"Paperwork? I hadn't thought of that. But, of course. Good idea." Odette walks over to her purse and grabs her laptop. Sitting back down, she opens her MacBook and pulls up a new document. "Obviously, my main concern is taking care of my parents."

"How do you feel about me paying the assisted living costs for ten years?"

Her eyebrows shoot up. "That's... a lot. Are you sure that's fair? If we're only going to stay married for a few years—"

"I think it's more than fair. You're doing me a massive favor. You're putting your entire life on hold for two years. Obviously, this isn't a romantic arrangement, but we'll still need to act like a loving couple in public, live together, all of it. I understand the sacrifice you're making."

She stops typing and looks up at me. "What exactly does *acting like a loving couple* entail?"

I clear my throat and squirm a bit in my seat. "Well, most married people show... affection. They naturally hold hands and, you know, probably kiss each other."

She blushes, though her gaze is sharp. "And what about at home? You know, in private."

"My apartment has two bedrooms. I was thinking that you could have the master and I'll take the guest room. There's even two bathrooms, so you'll have your own space. I have no... well, *physical expectations* of you in private."

She takes a deep breath. "Okay. That makes me feel better."

"Also, because of my trust fund and investments, as well as my father's, you'll have to sign a prenuptial agreement." She cringes, and I give her an empathetic look.

"I guess I should've expected that." She continues typing.

"What else should we add to the contract?"

"Well, I don't think we should date other people while we're married. It would be embarrassing if people thought my husband was being unfaithful to me. It would probably jeopardize your campaign as well." She glances at me briefly. "I feel awkward bringing up such a personal subject."

I lean across the table and close her laptop, so I have her undivided attention. "Odette, I wouldn't even think of seeing other women, whether this marriage is romantic or not." I'm trying to keep my voice calm and level, but I feel strongly about this. "I don't know if you remember Jennifer Briar from high school." Odette shakes her head. "We got engaged right after law school. Then she left me a year and a half ago for my old roommate. They had been seeing each other for over a year behind my back." I inhale a sharp breath. "Obviously I didn't handle it well... and I would never treat someone like that."

"I'm sorry. I didn't know."

"I just want you to know that, real or not, I take this marriage seriously."

Awkward silence settles between us for a few seconds before I change the subject. "What day would work for you to meet up and sign the documents?"

"Can we do it in a few days? I need to be here to help my dad settle back in."

"Of course." I wring my hands together. "And I'm sorry that we don't have more time to get to know each other. But since it's mid-December now and I'm announcing my campaign the first weekend in January, we'll have to marry within the next couple of weeks."

"That's okay. I knew everything would happen quickly."

Once dinner is over, she yawns. I'm sure she is exhausted, so I take the hint and help her clean up the meal.

As she walks me toward the door to say goodbye, I suddenly remember the book. "Oh! I nearly forgot. I have one more thing in my bag of tricks." I walk over to my bag by the coat rack and pull out the leather-bound copy of Pride and Prejudice. "This is my favorite romance. I mean, it's the only romance I've ever read, but I wanted you to have a copy in case you haven't read it. I'm expecting you to be the Elizabeth Bennett to my Fitzwilliam Darcy." I lean in close to her and whisper seriously, "So if you're not very accomplished at the pianoforte, you had better start practicing."

"Unless you own a mansion in the English countryside, don't count on it." She deadpans.

A boisterous laugh escapes my mouth, and she cracks a smile. Right before I walk out the door, I take her hand in mine and place a gentle kiss on the back of her hand. "Good night, my betrothed."

When I look up, I can't help but notice the goosebumps breaking out on her arm. A blush colors her cheeks. "You're taking this Mr.

Darcy thing way too seriously. Good night, Madden."

Chapter 10

Odette

♥

Three days after agreeing to marry Madden, my father came home from the hospital. Mom and I initiated the difficult discussion about selling the house and moving them both into assisted living. Dad put up a fight, of course, but deep down I think he knew it was the best choice.

Madden put us in contact with a great real estate agent, so Mom and I will be busy prepping the house for showings over the next few weeks, not to mention taking care of Dad until they both move into their assisted living duplex next week.

Amidst all the chaos, Mom and I also took care of the power of attorney paperwork. Since I'm officially in charge of their finances now, it's been far easier to cover up how we're paying for their duplex at Sunflower Assisted Living. I initially told her that Medicare is paying for it, but they actually only pay a small portion for the first 100 days. After that, Madden will pay for all of it.

Madden and I are on our way now to meet with his lawyer, and I've never been so anxious. I should've put some deodorant in my purse because my armpits currently think they're Niagara Falls. Once I sign on the dotted line, there's no going back.

Madden pulls up to a sleek, tall building in downtown Wichita and effortlessly parallel parks. Why is he so suave? Does good breeding guarantee good looks *and* parallel parking skills from the moment that you're born?

He gets out and walks around the car to open my door for me, taking my hand helpfully as I step out of the vehicle. When he lets go, I can't help but glance at his hand to see if he does Mr. Darcy's infamous hand stretch after helping Elizabeth Bennet into her carriage. He doesn't

We walk into the building and take the elevator up to Bennington & Associates on the top floor. We're both silent the entire ride up. Obviously, I'm not the only one feeling nervous. The elevator chirps as the doors open and we step out into a ritzy-looking office with modern furniture, glossy black desks, and probably a million dollars worth of Fiddle Leaf fig trees arranged throughout. Even the air smells fancy, like they order their hand soap and cleaning supplies from France or something.

A well-coiffed gentleman with grey hair walks toward us. He's not much taller than I am, but his confident stride and expensive-looking suit make me think he must be in charge here.

"Madden! Great to see you." He reaches out and shakes Madden's hand. He turns his brown eyes toward me. "And this lovely young lady must be Odette?"

"My fiancée, Odette Hastings." Madden introduces me with a smile.

"Richard Bennington. I'm very pleased to meet you, Odette." The man gives my hand a gentle handshake. He gestures toward the long hallway. "Shall we all head back to the conference room and get started?"

Madden gives me a reassuring smile, then turns back to Richard. "Of course, we'll follow you."

As we walk down the long hallway, I begin to feel as though the walls are closing in on me, like one of those ancient corridors in

Raiders of The Lost Ark. My throat tightens and my mouth goes dry. Madden looks over at me and, probably noticing my panicked expression, puts his hand on the small of my back. I know he means it as a comforting gesture, but instead, it makes me feel warm all over. I begin to sweat even more.

Just as we're about to reach the conference room, a man pokes his head out of one of the nearby offices. He's boyishly handsome, with brown curls resting on his forehead, blue eyes, and a dimple in his chin. "Oh, Madden! So glad I get to meet the future Mrs!" His tone is a little too enthusiastic to sound genuine.

Madden stiffens next to me. "Odette, this is Christopher Highman."

I nod. "Nice to meet you."

"As a partner here, I really miss Madden's excellent skills at filing paperwork," He says condescendingly. I quirk an eyebrow.

Richard looks at Christopher with an annoyed expression. "If you don't mind, we have some important paperwork to take care of."

"Of course. Sorry to interrupt such important business." He sneers.

Madden ignores Christopher's comment as Richard leads us into a conference room. I can't help but wonder why there's so much tension between Madden and this Christopher guy. I've never heard anyone speak to Madden with anything but respect in their voice.

The conference room that Richard leads us into is bare aside from a long table in the center surrounded by leather office chairs. We all take our seats at the very end of the grand table where a laptop and a thick folder rest.

Richard folds his hands together and looks at Madden and I. "Madden already informed me that you're both aware of the terms of your marriage. He emailed me the document you created together, and I simply cleaned it up and added all the necessary legal jargon to make it official. So, today, we're here to make sure that there's nothing else either of you might want to add into the contract. We will also go over the prenuptial agreement and the nondisclosure agreement." He opens his laptop and clicks open a document. "Let's start with the contract and we'll do the signatures last."

I flush with embarrassment. Richard must think we're insane. Madden doesn't seem worried, though, and simply nods.

"Perfect. Then allow me to summarize what I have so far." He clears his throat and reads aloud from his laptop.

"Item one: The marriage of Madden Windell and Odette Hastings will end in one year in the case Madden is not elected into Congress. In the case that Madden *is* elected into Congress, the marriage will end in two years.

Item two: Mr. Windell agrees to pay for the care and living arrangements of Mr. and Mrs. Hastings for the next ten years.

Item three: In the case Mr. Windell seeks reelection after his first Congressional term and Odette Hastings agrees to add two more years onto this contract, Mr. Windell agrees to pay a bonus of $50,000 per year to Miss Hastings upon signing a new contract.

Item four: Odette Hastings will be provided a private bedroom and bathroom during the course of this marriage."

Richard pauses and looks at us. "How does this sound so far?"

I raise my eyebrows in question as I whip my head over to look at Madden. "Wait, what's this about two extra years?"

"Sorry, I should've mentioned this the other night. Most Congressmen seek reelection at the end of their term. But as you heard, that's something we can add onto the contract later, if we decide to."

I take a deep breath. "Okay. As long as I don't have to agree to four years right this second."

"No, of course not. I wouldn't ask that of you."

Richard prints the contract once we both confirm the terms, then we move onto the nondisclosure agreement. Richard opens the thick folder laying next to him and pulls out a packet held together by a large paperclip.

"The nondisclosure agreement simply states that everything we've talked about in this office today stays private. Anyone you told before today doesn't affect the agreement; I understand that Madden's family already knows about the situation. By signing this form, you acknowledge the risk that exposure could threaten each of your public images as well as Madden's political campaign. The fewer people who know, the better." He lays the papers before us, marked with sticky tabs, showing us where to sign.

Next, we sign the prenup, which makes my skin crawl. Richard explains prenups are typical when there's a trust fund involved. Up until three nights ago, I had no clue Madden and his siblings had trust funds. His world is definitely very different from mine.

Lastly, we come up with a convincing story to tell the public. I've rehearsed it in my mind so many times over the last few hours that I'm confident I can keep it straight.

In our fake story, we bumped into each other during one of Madden's trips to D.C. last year. Once I moved back to Wichita, we saw each other at the reunion and then again at Thanksgiving, and that was all it took to rekindle the romance. We knew we were in love. We wanted to get married right away so we could have some time together before his campaign schedule gets crazy.

We will announce our engagement to my parents and to the local newspapers–as well as on Madden's website–within the next few days.

Unease stirs in my stomach. This is going to come as a tremendous shock to my parents, but I hope we can convince them that Madden and I are in love. They can never find out that I did this to pay for

Dad's care or they would feel horrible. Lying leaves a pit in my stomach, but I shove the feeling down. This is for the greater good.

Now all I need to do is convince the world I'm in love with Madden Windell.

Chapter 11

Madden

♥

W alking up to my parents' door, I square my shoulders and brace myself for Mom's reaction to my impending marriage to Odette. I know she wasn't really on board with me marrying someone who's not in our social circle and doesn't come from money, but she's just going to have to get over it.

I imagine this news will go over very differently here than it did at the Hastings' home this morning. Odette's parents looked a little confused when we told them about our quick engagement, but they hugged me and still seemed ecstatic to welcome me into their family. Overall, they seemed happy for us. Apparently, their own engagement decades ago was pretty short also, though still not as short as ours— and they were also 45 when they got engaged and not 28. But still, I'm glad they're not suspicious.

Swinging my parents' front door open, I stride inside to the living room, where I can hear Mom typing away on her laptop. She looks up as I enter and smiles. "Well, what a surprise! To what do I owe the pleasure of seeing my eldest son?"

I chuckle and roll my eyes at her formality. "I have a bit of an announcement, actually. Is Dad home, too?"

She closes her laptop and jumps up from her seat. "*Ted*! Madden has an announcement!"

I hear my Dad grumbling as he saunters into the living room. "Make this quick. I'm watching golf."

"Yes, you're obviously a busy person." She states bitterly.

They scowl at each other, and I clear my throat to draw their attention back to me. "I'm engaged to Odette Hastings. She knows the reason for our marriage and we already signed the paperwork with Richard Bennington to make it official. She's going to rescue my campaign."

Mom's mouth gapes open for a moment, then snaps closed. "Odette? What happened to Heidi?"

"Heidi? You can't be serious. She brings her yappy dog with her everywhere she goes!" I say with a groan.

"But she has connections that could've helped your campaign!"

"Stop trying to control his decisions, Diane. You're being ridiculous." Dad crosses his arms.

"Oh, so now I'm controlling?"

I hold my hands out in front of me like a referee. "Okay, okay. Let's calm down. This marriage isn't forever. It's practically a business arrangement." I rub the back of my neck. "I know you're not thrilled about my choice, Mom, but I'm going to need your expert event-planning abilities for the wedding... which is the weekend after Christmas."

"That's in a week and a half!"

"But this is your superpower. You could plan a wedding in less time, I know you could." I'm kissing up to win her over, but I'm desperate. If Odette and I are going to convince anyone that our marriage is real, it has to *look* real. A courthouse ceremony won't cut it.

"This is extremely inconvenient. Do you have any idea what you're asking?" Mom wrinkles her nose in disgust. But after a few seconds, she begrudgingly agrees. "Fine. Does she have a dress yet? Tell me that she didn't go pick one up from a thrift shop."

"Stop. Odette is perfectly capable of choosing a wedding gown." I shoot her an annoyed glance.

"If you say so. But I know an excellent shop downtown. I will make an appointment ASAP."

"Thank you." I start towards the door but then turn back to hand her my Visa. "You can charge it to my credit card, but *please* don't go too crazy. And be nice to my fiancée."

⇜

Odette

Mrs. Windell is a party-planner extraordinaire. Decorating and making things look fancy definitely isn't my area of expertise, so I'm relieved that I don't have to do any of it. As long as my dad is there to walk me down the aisle–walker and all–I'll be happy.

It's one week before my wedding day and I'm currently hyperventilating in my car outside a wedding dress boutique in downtown Wichita. I've always hated being the center of attention, so the thought of trying on dresses in front of my mom, Kate, and Madden's mom is intimidating. I'm so absorbed by my thoughts that when Kate taps my driver's side window, I almost jump out of my skin.

She doubles over laughing and yanks my car door open. "Are you going to sit out here forever or are you going to come inside and wow us with how beautiful you look in these wedding gowns?"

I step out of the car, and she pulls me into a hug, probably sensing my anxiety. "You know I hate being the center of attention like this. Can't you try on the dresses and I'll just pick my favorite?" I slump my shoulders.

"Listen, I'm sure this past week has been a lot. You got engaged to *Madden Windell*. Try to enjoy today, okay? Wedding dress shopping is the best part of the whole process!" Kate throws her arm around my shoulders as we walk.

"I don't know why we can't just wear jeans and go to the courthouse."

"Come on! You're marrying a total hottie. He's going to be blown away when he sees you walking down the aisle." She swoons. "I'm so excited for you."

I attempt a genuine smile, since she doesn't know that Madden and I aren't really in love. "You're right. This is the only fun thing I've gotten to do all week. Let's get in there and pick out a wedding dress!"

We give each other a high five the Olsen twins would envy.

"That's my girl!" Kate exclaims.

I spend the next two hours trying on wedding dress after wedding dress. Each time I'm zipped into another dress, my entourage "oohs" and "ahhs" as I come to stand on the little stage. Most of the dresses are fine, but the last one I tried on was horrendous: I looked like a cupcake covered in rhinestones and taffeta. At least we had a good laugh about it. Everyone except Mrs. Windell, at least. I'm pretty sure that one was her favorite.

None of them feel right until I slip on the very last dress. I'm fairly certain that Madden's mom put it at the bottom of the pile because it's too understated for her taste, but once I put it on, the sleek chiffon floats over my body like it was made for me. I'm instantly in love.

I glide out in front of my little audience. Despite the simplicity of the gown, their jaws drop and my mom's eyes fill with tears.

I take in my reflection as I stand in front of the large mirror. The slightly off-white color of the dress compliments my pale skin beautifully. The top is sleek and has a deep, square neckline, and the fabric cinches in at my waist, accentuating the slenderest part of me. Opaque sleeves gracefully flutter away from my arms and then come into lace cuffs at my wrists, making me feel like a medieval princess. There's a very slight train in the back completing the dress perfectly.

Part of me hates to choose such a perfect dress for a fake marriage. Tears sting my eyes at the bittersweetness of the moment. I'm finally a bride, but it isn't real. When I used to picture my wedding, I didn't think much about the dress or the flowers; all I pictured was the man at the opposite end of the aisle looking at me like I was the only person in the entire universe. I seriously doubt that Madden will look at me that way.

Regardless, I need a dress, and we all wholeheartedly agree that this is the one. We spend a bit more time browsing accessories, and I decide on a simple headpiece that looks like gold vines weaving throughout my hair. For my shoes, I'll wear the white satin slippers my mother wore when she married my father. At least that part of my wedding will be real.

Kate walks my mom to the car as Mrs. Windell and I stay back to pay. Suddenly, a thought hits me: I have no idea what Madden expects me to wear. What if the dress isn't formal enough for him? Will it convey the right message to the public?

Mrs. Windell notices my facial expression. "What is it, dear? You look upset."

I hesitate, biting my bottom lip. "It's just... What if Madden doesn't like the dress?"

She seems surprised by my question. She cocks her head to the side and puts her hands on her hips. "Let me tell you something about my son: He couldn't care less about fancy wedding gowns. His father set him up with all the wealthiest and most eligible young ladies these past six months and he didn't feel a connection with *any* of them." She rolls her eyes and continues, "He could've chosen a glamorous girl who would've worn a magnificent designer gown down the aisle, but he didn't. He obviously thinks there is something special about you, even if he hasn't admitted that to himself yet. Men can be a little clueless sometimes." She pats my shoulder.

By her words, I have a feeling she might have preferred it if Madden chose one of those more glamorous women, but her strange pep talk did manage to make me feel a little better.

Chapter 12

Madden

♥

Only a week and a half after announcing our engagement, it's the night before my wedding. We're at my makeshift bachelor party, just my dad, my brothers, and Paul. The last few weeks have been exhausting–what with wedding plans, moving Odette's parents, and Christmas–so I'm more than happy that tonight is a low-key affair. All I needed was a good steak, some expensive bourbon, and a relaxing soak in a hot tub. Nothing crazy, but you never know what to expect when Brooks is involved.

The closer we get to my wedding day, the more nervous I am. Marriage is a big deal. Part of me always thought that if I ended up getting married, it would be for life. But I suppose it's better to end things amicably after a few years than to be in a miserable marriage forever. I've seen first-hand what that might be like.

"Well, it's your last night as a single man!" Brooks claps me on the back. "Sorry, you have to spend it with a bunch of ugly men. Excluding myself, of course."

I dunk him under the water in David's hot tub because he's annoying. And I felt like it.

"Are you ready for tomorrow?" Dad glances at me before taking a sip of bourbon.

"Who wouldn't be ready to marry a fox like Odette?" Brooks winks at me and tries to get a high five from David, but my middle brother just ignores him.

He turns to Dad and asks, "Do you think you could give me that list of trust-fund babes you gave Madden? I'll need a wife, eventually."

This time Dad dunks him under the water. When he comes spluttering back up Dad drawls, "I plan to keep you from getting married for as long as possible."

We all nod in agreement.

"I think I'm as ready for tomorrow as I possibly can be. I'm definitely nervous, though." I run my hands through my wet hair.

Brooks drops his head down dramatically in mock frustration. "Aw, Dad, don't tell me that you haven't had *the talk* with him yet. About the birds and the bees? It's okay to be a little nervous, bro."

This time, David dunks him under the water. Three out of three.

"Every man is nervous the night before his wedding. Even if they're actually in love with the person they're marrying," Paul says with a smile.

David refills his bourbon glass. "What are the girls up to tonight?"

"They're having wine at Odette's best friend's house. They even invited Sophie. I'm glad she could fly home for this." I smile fondly. I've missed my sister; we're the closest in age, so it was important to me to have her here.

Dad nods. "It was hard for Soph to send Sam off on his deployment, so it was awfully nice for them to include her. Did you see how Sophie's face lit up when Odette asked her to be a bridesmaid?"

The edges of my lips pull up into a smile. "Odette is a wonderful woman."

My throat tightens. Too wonderful to be stuck in a loveless marriage. For her sake, I hope this campaign goes quickly.

Odette

"Okay, ladies, what are we feeling tonight? *The Wedding Planner, The Wedding Date*, or *My Best Friend's Wedding*?" Kate jiggles the TV remote excitedly.

"How do we decide between Dermot Mulroney and Matthew McConaughey?" Madden's sister, Sophie, whistles as she sets the bowl of popcorn on the coffee table and plays with her long braid.

I study her for a moment. She has grown up since I saw her in high school. She's like a prettier female version of Madden and Brooks, with her shiny blonde hair and sparkly blue eyes. She has that whole *girl next door* look going for her.

"Can't we watch a documentary or something educational instead?" I shove a handful of popcorn in my mouth.

"Oh! I almost forgot!" Kate takes off into the kitchen and comes back carrying a glossy black bag filled with hot pink tissue paper.

"Oh, my word, Kate. Why don't you just wait and give this to us at the wedding?" I take the gift from her cautiously.

"Trust me. You'll want to open this in private." Kate giggles.

I toss the bag off my lap like it's on fire. "Oh, no. I'm not opening this."

"Please open it! I'm terribly curious now." Sophie picks up the mysterious bag off the floor and sets it back on my lap. She obviously doesn't know Kate very well or she definitely wouldn't want me to open it.

After taking several gulps of my wine, I slowly lift the tissue paper away. When I pull out the item from the bottom of the gift bag, I'm stuck holding a light pink see-through negligee with matching underwear. Although, really, there's hardly enough fabric to consider it underwear.

Kate waggles her eyebrows at me as I glare back at her. Poor Sophie just blushes and looks down at her feet awkwardly.

"Wow, thanks. I'm sure Madden will love it." I toss it back in the bag and feel my cheeks flaming. Of course she bought me lingerie. She doesn't know that there's no chance of Madden seeing me naked anytime this century.

Kate laughs. "Don't be embarrassed! I lied when I told you that picking out the wedding dress is the best part. That distinction belongs to the wedding night."

"Why don't we spare Sophie all this talk about her brother's wedding night? I'm sure that's the last thing she wants to talk about." I look at Kate pointedly. She has no filter, and Sophie looks extremely uncomfortable. Really, though, I just want to spare myself.

Sophie changes the subject. "I'm pretty stoked to get a sister-in-law! I didn't think Madden would ever consider marriage again after the whole thing with his ex. You must have converted him."

I smile. "Yeah, it will be nice to have siblings. Maybe we could visit you and Sam once he gets back?" I was trying to be positive, but Sophie's face falls at the reminder of her husband's deployment.

"I'm so sorry he has to be away. That must be so difficult." Kate gives her an empathetic smile. "Have some wine. That makes everything better."

Sophie awkwardly shoos Kate's offered wine glass away. "No, thank you. Just water for me."

Mine and Kate's jaws drop. "Are you pregnant?" We exclaim in unison.

"Well, yes...." Sophie's face turns bright red. "I'm so sorry, Odette. I wasn't going to say anything until after the wedding. I don't want to make this weekend about me."

"Nonsense, I'm so happy for you!" And I have no problem with her making this weekend about something other than my fake wedding. Her news is a welcome distraction.

"Thank you." She gives me a sweet smile. "Sam will still be in Afghanistan when I give birth, since his deployment is nine months long." Her eyes fill with tears and she fans her hands in front of her face furiously. "I don't mean to cry. It's the hormones."

"Girl, you cry all you want to." Kate hands her a box of tissues.

We sit on either side of Sophie and cover ourselves in a sea of fluffy blankets. The three of us agree to watch *Baby Mama* in honor of her joyful news, and we spend the rest of our evening pretending Amy Poehler and Tina Fey are our best friends.

Okay, maybe that last part is just me.

Chapter 13

Madden

♥

My heart is racing a thousand miles a minute as I walk to the front of my parent's church and take my place next to the pastor. The thought of marrying someone who's basically a stranger feels all too real this morning. I can't believe I'm actually doing this. My stomach is bordering somewhere between flying into space or emptying all of its contents. I take a deep breath and discreetly wipe my sweaty palms on the sides of my tuxedo jacket.

There are maybe fifty guests here: just close friends, family, and some of the people on my campaign team who could make it. My parents and Odette's mom are dressed to the nines and looking quite pleased. Even my mother, waving to me happily from the front pew, seems to have settled down about me and Odette getting married.

She did a lovely job with the decor. Not that I'd expect anything less. The woman clearly missed her calling as an event planner. The aisles are lined with garlands of dark greenery interspersed with some spriggy-looking plant–wheat stalks, maybe? Behind me, there's a circular arch covered with flowers in various shades of dark red, gold, and white overlooking the altar. The entire chapel is truly ethereal. I hope Odette will be pleased with the decor.

The whole church quiets down when the pianist softly begins playing *Canon in D*. The first to walk down the aisle are Brooks and Sophie, looking so much alike that they could be twins. They take their places on stage, and then David and Kate follow suit. My brothers wear black tuxes that match mine, only their ties are dark red and mine is white. Kate and Sophie have on long, velvet dresses that perfectly match my brothers' red ties.

How on earth did Mom put all of this together in two weeks? What sorcery is this?

I'm pulled from my thoughts when the wedding march begins and everyone stands, awaiting the grand entrance of the bride.

My bride.

Odette enters beside her father at the other end of the aisle and they begin their slow procession toward me. Mr. Hastings holds his own well enough with his walker in hand, but definitely slower since the surgery. I'm just grateful that he's able to be here for Odette today.

My eyes travel back to Odette, and I can tell from all the way over here that she's absolutely stunning. The closer they get, the more details I make out. Her bouquet matches the flowers in the awning behind me and her hair is twisted back into a cascade of luscious curls with a headband resembling a gold vine weaving through it. Her dress is simple, but it outlines her slim figure, and the neckline dips down just enough to be incredibly sexy but still sophisticated. She looks exquisite. I've never seen her in something so form-fitting.

I discreetly pinch my leg through the fabric of my suit, trying to distract myself from ogling her gorgeous figure. This is a business arrangement and nothing more. I don't want to make it weird.

I meet Odette and Mr. Hastings at the front of the aisle. A tear runs down his cheek as he gives Odette a kiss and pats my shoulder, then takes his seat next to his wife, who's already crying.

Odette clasps my outstretched hand and I can tell immediately that hers are just as clammy as mine. We slowly make our way up the steps to the pastor.

The ceremony feels like an out-of-body experience, partly because I'm nervous, and partly because I can't believe I'm getting married to someone I hardly know. But what I *do* know is she's lovely and kind. The fact that she is willing to marry me is a miracle. Yet here she is.

Before I know it, the pastor announces us as husband and wife. He looks at me with a wink and says that I may kiss my bride. I freeze. I hadn't thought about this part. *How did I not think about this part?*

I mean, of course, I've thought about kissing her, but I usually pictured us at a campaign event or something. This feels far more intimate. I guess one might consider it to be a case of public affection, and that's in the contract. Should I give her a peck on the cheek, a passionate kiss where I dip her back, or something in between? What would look more natural, more *real*?

I have to think fast. Not only is everyone is waiting, but Odette is watching my face in confusion.

What the heck. I'm going for it. Who knows when I'll get to kiss her again?

I find her shiny, pink lips suddenly irresistible. I hear her suck in a breath when I step forward and slide one hand around her waist, then use my other hand to cup her chin. My lips meet hers, softly at first, and then I lean my head slightly to deepen the kiss. Much to my surprise, she melts against me and slips her hands around my neck. Definitely wasn't expecting that. My heart jumps.

And she was worried that she wouldn't be a good actress! If I didn't know better, I definitely would think this is a real kiss.

We slowly pull back, both of us looking a little stunned. When I link her arm through mine, her face turns the darkest shade of red I've had the privilege to see so far.

The guests cheer and we walk down the aisle together as Stevie Wonder's "For Once In My Life" plays behind us.

Odette

What on earth just happened?

Was that a genuine kiss or a fake kiss? Maybe Madden is just a really good actor? Everyone surrounds us, giving hugs and congratulations, but I can't take my eyes off of my husband.

Oh, my gosh, I have a husband. And why does the man have to look so good in a tux?

Kate interrupts my not-so-innocent thoughts as she pulls me into a big hug and whispers, "That was some kiss. Betcha' can't wait to slip on the present I gave you last night!"

I don't even have to look at her to know that she's waggling her eyebrows.

The rest of the day passes quickly with photos and the reception. We had a simple, small wedding and it was perfect. I couldn't have planned a better wedding if I would've had twelve months instead of two weeks. Mrs. Windell is obviously some kind of miracle worker. Eventually, the festivities come to an end and our small crowd of friends and family see us off.

Once we're alone in Madden's Audi, I suddenly feel uncomfortable. It's so quiet that every tiny movement I make seems amplified. The tension is thick, like when it's extremely humid outside and the air makes it difficult to breathe. Thankfully, Madden's place isn't far and soon enough we pull into a parking spot right next to Dad's old Buick. My parents dropped it off yesterday "in case I need it". I feel embarrassed by how junky it looks parked next to all the new, shiny vehicles nearby. I move to open the car door, but Madden turns to me and gently touches my arm.

"Odette, wait." He swallows and takes a deep breath. "I can't let this day go by without telling you what an absolutely beautiful bride you are." His eyes are so sincere that I can't look away.

The only response I seem capable of is a whispered, "Thank you."

Madden and his brothers moved my things over yesterday while my Mom and I got our nails done, so we have very little to carry in now. Madden steps out of the car and comes around to open the door for me, and then we silently walk up the path to the brick apartment complex. Coming inside, I follow Madden to the elevator and we ride up, floor after floor, in a strange silence. Neither of us knows what to say.

I breathe a sigh of relief when the elevator doors finally open at the very top floor. We step into a short, wide hallway with only one door at the end. Madden leads me to the apartment door and opens it for me. To my relief, he doesn't offer to carry me over the threshold.

I walk into the most pristine home I've ever had the pleasure of seeing. There's a brown leather sectional, a big flat-screen TV, a few pieces of modern art on the walls, and no clutter whatsoever. I turn into the dining area, and that's when I spot an out-of-place picture on the wall above the table. I look over at Madden and he can barely contain his laughter, so of course, I laugh right along with him.

The picture is a watercolor painting of the English countryside with a mansion at the center. A small plaque at the bottom of the frame reads, "This is Our Pemberley." Obviously, a nod to the start of our lives as Mr. Darcy and Elizabeth Bennett.

Except they were actually in love. "I saw it online, and I just had to get it." He stuffs his hands into his pockets like a little boy.

I laugh and touch his arm. "It's perfect. Thank you for the laugh."

After an awkward pause, Madden removes his hands from his pockets and rubs them together. "Well, Mrs. Windell, let me lead you to your chamber." He bows and then gestures down the hallway to the master bedroom.

All of my bags are already inside. The room looks very cozy with a king-sized bed, fluffy white comforter, lavender candles on the nightstands, and pretty brass lamps. There's a spacious closet in the corner and an attached bathroom with a walk-in, marble shower, and a giant bathtub that I'll definitely take advantage of later tonight. I smile and nod approvingly. "Wow, Madden. This place is awesome." I clear my throat. "And where's the guest room?"

He has his hands in his pockets again but pulls one out to run it through his hair. "It's just down this hallway, along with the guest bathroom. So I won't ever have to bother you." He laughs nervously.

I bite my lip. Having Madden Windell as my roommate already feels weirder than I thought it would. "Right. Well, I'm just going to get settled in and probably jump in the shower."

"Sure, okay. I hope you sleep well. I know it's been a long day." He leaves quietly and closes the door behind him.

Chapter 14

Madden

♥

*D*o not think about Odette in the shower, I repeat; do not think about Odette in the shower. You're not a perv, Madden. You can handle this.

I smother myself with my pillow as I lay on my new bed in the guest room, repeating this mantra and trying not to smell the delicious aroma of her shampoo currently wafting through the entire apartment.

This is fine. Everything is fine. I can live platonically with my gorgeous wife–er, roommate–while keeping my hands to myself. No biggie.

I let out a loud groan and dramatically scrub my hands down my face. The *idea* of living with Odette didn't seem like such a big deal, but now that she's here in person and I can smell her and see her, and I know she's sleeping just down the hallway... it's much more tempting than I'd imagined.

I just have to get through the day tomorrow. After that, it'll be Monday and we'll announce my campaign at a press conference. Then we'll get busy hitting the campaign trail hard. Throwing myself into campaigning is just the distraction I need to keep myself from thinking about Odette.

After making a campaign to-do list in my head, I eventually drift off to sleep.

At 6:00 AM the next morning (on the dot), I wake up as usual. I've always been a morning person, but I'm especially thankful for that today as I'll have the chance to move around before I come face to face with my wife. I go straight to the guest bathroom to take a hot shower, then dress in a t-shirt and the comfy llama pants Odette's mom got me for Christmas. I walk down the hallway to the kitchen to brew some coffee. Entering the living room, though, I come upon a sight that stops me dead in my tracks.

Odette is doing yoga. In tiny yoga shorts and a tank top.

Jesus, take the wheel. I can't do this. I turn and silently bang my head against the wall.

"Good morning! Uh, Madden? You okay?" Odette has come out of her warrior pose and stares at me with concern.

"Yes, of course." I squeak out. "This is just how I wake up in the mornings."

"By banging your head against the wall?" She looks at me like someone should send me to an insane asylum. Frankly, someone probably should.

"Yep. I read about it in one of those self-help books. Gets the blood pumping." I'm going to need to read a lot more self-help books. I slap a charming smile on my face, but I probably look like a doofus. "Would you like some coffee?"

"Yes, please," she looks down awkwardly and crosses her arms. "Sorry if I interrupted your routine. I always start my mornings with yoga."

"No, you're fine. I'm glad that you're making yourself at home," I say with a smile. "On weekdays I go down to the gym, but I skip it on the weekends. You're welcome to use the gym at the community center as well." And then I won't have to see you in your yoga shorts.

We head into the kitchen, and I start the coffee while Odette scrambles some eggs and bacon. It feels a little odd to have another person here; I have to admit. Jen and I never lived together, so I've been on my own since graduating from law school. I was comfortable with the solitude, but it's also kind of nice to have company in this big apartment.

Over our breakfast, we pull out our phone calendars and go over my campaign schedule for the next few weeks. "Tomorrow is the press conference where I'll announce my campaign to the public, and then on Wednesday, I have a speaking event at Wichita State University. It would be great if you could come with me to those. Oh, and my campaign team will help me hand out fliers this weekend."

"And so it begins." Odette smirks. She adds the events to her calendar. "Those should work. I would like to make it to see my parents every morning, but if there are any morning events this week, I can see them in the afternoon instead."

She sighs and bites her bottom lip nervously. "It's a little weird to sync our schedules like this, huh?"

I chuckle and run my hand through my hair. "It really is. I'm not used to planning around another person."

"Well, I suppose we'll get used to it, eventually?" She shrugs.

Scrolling through my Google calendar, I notice we have a few free evenings. "Hey, what if we try to fit in some time together each week? If we have to live together, we might as well get to know each other, right?

"True." She smiles. "Sounds good to me."

I rub the back of my neck and take a deep breath. "Once we get past the primaries in August, we can breathe, at least. These next nine months are going to be intense. Are you ready for it?"

She quirks an eyebrow at me. "Don't forget that assisting politicians was my full-time job. I've missed it, actually. It'll all be worth it when you're a Congressman."

I lean against the kitchen wall with my coffee mug in hand. "You really think I can win?"

She chuckles. "Of course! You're one of the good ones. You're genuine, kind, and you want to help. The voters can sense that." She pauses, then smirks. "Why else would I agree to marry you?"

Because of my high-handed financial assistance. I push the thought away and wink at her. "My dazzling good looks, of course."

"I *am* a sucker for a man who wears llama pajama pants."

Surprised by her quick comeback, I belt out a laugh. She gives me a humorous pat on the back as she walks past me, back to her room.

Trying not to notice the way her hips sway in her little shorts, I glance down at my phone and see that I missed several texts from my family group chat. I roll my eyes and scroll through the messages.

Brooks: Madden, I have to know: did you figure out the whole "birds and bees" thing?

David: Brooks, leave him alone.

Sophie: Hey, Madden, you missed my announcement last night: Sam and I are expecting!

Brooks: Such amazing news. Chicks dig babies. It can be my little wingman/woman.

Dad: You will not use my grandchild to pick up women.

Me: Brooks, you're ridiculous. *GIF of Robert Downey Jr. crossing his arms and rolling his eyes*

Me: And congrats, Sophie! That's awesome.

~⚡~

Odette

Only Madden could wear flannel pants with Santa-hat-clad llamas plastered all over them and still look sexy. It's infuriating. And his t-shirt? Why even wear a shirt if it's so tight that I can see every chiseled muscle underneath?

I shake my head. The campaign. Focus on the campaign. That's what I'm here for.

This year is going to be insanely busy. I'll probably need to go shopping soon for a few outfits and dresses to wear to events. Shopping is not my area of expertise, so Kate will have to come with me. I shoot her a text while I'm thinking about it.

Me: Good morning!

Kate: Good morning. ;) How was last night?

Me: Hot and steamy... thanks to the best shower of my life. The hot water in this apartment is outstanding.

Kate: Not funny.

Me: A lady never kisses and tells. Anyway, I need to acquire the wardrobe of a politician's wife. Will you style me?

Kate: I'm seeing pantsuits. Lots of pantsuits. A rainbow of pantsuits!

Me: How about less Hillary and more Michelle or Melania?

Kate: Gotcha. Let's go this week since I'm still on Christmas break!

Me: That'll be perfect. Sophie flies back to North Carolina on Friday. So how about Thursday so she can come with us?

Kate: I have it in my calendar! We'll have you looking like Jackie O. in no time.

With no reason to look sexy, I throw on some black leggings and my comfy Liberty University hoodie from college, then stride back out into the living room. Madden is on the sectional with the remote in-hand and a bowl of freshly popped popcorn on the coffee table in front of him.

"Today is the calm before the campaign storm, so why don't we enjoy it and watch some TV?" He asks.

I bite my bottom lip and think about it for a few seconds. "How about *Parks and Recreation*? Or is that too silly?"

His face lights up. "I love *Parks and Rec*. Leslie Knope and Ron Swanson make the perfect team."

"Agreed!" I snuggle onto the sofa at an appropriate distance from Madden and grab a handful of popcorn.

After watching a few episodes in comfortable silence, Madden turns to me abruptly. "If you were a combination of any two *Parks and Rec* characters, which ones would you be and why?

I take a moment to ponder, looking up at the ceiling. "Man, that's a difficult question. Probably Anne, because I like to think I'm a loyal friend like her. And also Leslie Knope because she's super organized and loves politics." I smile. "How about you?"

"I'm definitely an even mixture of Leslie and Tom. Leslie is your classic overachiever, and Tom is charismatic and loves the finer things in life." He smirks.

"Oh, you think you're charismatic, huh?" I raise an eyebrow and then smile to show him that I'm teasing. "That seems pretty accurate, at least from what I've seen so far."

He laughs. "Neither of us are Ron Swanson, though?"

"Unless one of us secretly hates the government, I think not."

"Good point. From what I can tell, though, Anne is pretty accurate for you. Maybe you should treat yourself once in a while, like Tom or Donna.".

I realize at this moment that, compared to his mom and girls like Heidi, I must seem very low maintenance. "Yeah, I'm definitely not great at treating myself."

"Maybe you can teach me to be more humble, like Anne, and I can teach you to spoil yourself once in a while, like Tom?"

I eye the personal massage chair sitting next to Madden's sofa. "Yeah, it doesn't appear that you have any trouble treating yourself."

He bursts out laughing. His laugh is big and fills the entire room, and I can't help but laugh right along with him. If I saw a picture of Madden smiling, I'd be able to hear his laugh ringing clearly in my head just from the photo.

We spend most of the day binge-watching the entire first season of *Parks and Recreation* and eventually order takeout.

As relaxing and enjoyable as our day has been, my heart squeezes when I think that there will never be more to our relationship than this. But isn't that what I signed up for: a loveless, transactional arrangement? I suppose I'm lucky that we even get along at all.

Chapter 15

Odette

♥

T he next morning, I'm seated shotgun in Madden's Audi while we drive to the city courthouse for Madden's campaign announcement.

Madden looks ever the politician in his crisp, black suit–tailored perfectly to fit his broad shoulders and narrow waist–and his eyes pop even more than usual against his indigo tie. He gelled his hair and combed it to the side this morning, which makes him look older and more distinguished.

Forget about Congress; he looks ready to become the president of the United States.

Next to him, I feel a little mousy. I curled my hair and threw on a serviceable pencil skirt since I haven't gone shopping with Kate and Sophie yet, but I'm self-conscious that people will look at my plain attire and wonder why on earth this dashing man married me.

Madden pulls into a parking spot outside the courthouse and then walks around to open my door for me. I smooth my skirt and tug on my tweed jacket as I step out of the car, making sure it all looks perfect. Madden must notice how anxious and fidgety I am because he gently puts his hand on the small of my back as we walk. Between the slight physical contact and the breeze blowing the smell of his cologne into my face, though, I'm pretty positive that I'll pass out from nerves any minute now.

"Don't worry. You look great." Madden flashes a charming grin.

I close my eyes and take a slow, deep breath. "I don't know why I'm so anxious. I knew what I signed up for, but pretending makes me feel like a fraud. You're not at all worried that people will find out?"

He looks at me with wide, anxious eyes. "If your parents believed us, why wouldn't strangers? Just relax and try to act natural. You won't even have to speak. Just hold on to my arm when we're in front of the cameras and smile at the crowd."

"I guess I can do that." I gaze up at him briefly and manage to trip over my own feet in the process.

"You okay?" Madden asks tersely. Is he annoyed at how anxious and ungraceful I am today? Or is he just as nervous as I am?

"Yep. Just great."

Inside the courthouse, several reporters and cameramen from different local TV stations flank the press stand. Paul Newhouse and Madden's family are already at the front of the large room. Once we reach them, Dr. Windell pats Madden on the back, his eyes filled with pride. Mrs. Windell looks incredible in her fitted, navy-blue sheath dress. I realize with an internal groan that I should've asked her to style me for this.

"Did you go over the speech we prepared?" Paul asks.

"Of course." Madden pulls a small stack of notecards out from his suit pocket.

Paul takes the cards from Madden and asks him to go over his speech a few times, just to be safe. While they're preoccupied, Sophie walks over to my side.

"Hey," she whispers. "Has my brother been a gentleman?"

I respond quietly, "He is. He gave me the master bedroom and moved his things to the guest room."

"I know we couldn't talk about this the night before the wedding, not in front of Kate. But I'm sorry that my brother talked you into this crazy idea." She looks around to make sure no one is listening.

"I was crazy enough to accept it, so I'm not much better than him." I shrug. "I was willing to do anything to take care of my parents. And it's only for a couple of years."

"They're lucky to have a daughter who would put her whole life on hold like this." She furrows her brow in concern.

Before I can respond, one of the journalists announces that we're going live in five minutes. I give Sophie a hesitant smile, then walk back to Madden's side.

I take Madden's offered arm as I approach. He seems perfectly at ease, even though he's moments away from appearing on live television.

He pats my hand and leans in to whisper, "Just take a deep breath."

The cameraman counts down, and we step up onto the small platform at the head of the room. Madden smiles like Prince Charming and waves at the cameras with confident ease, while I'm sure I look like a terrified deer about to become roadkill. Bright lights from the cameras flash all around us, and the small crowd of clapping reporters rings in my ears. I vaguely hear someone introduce Madden. He starts talking.

And then my brain effectively shuts off. I don't hear a word of his speech. It's like the information overload cut power to my senses. I completely zone out.

Only a few short minutes later, Madden wraps things up and clears his throat to bring me back to reality. He finished. We're done.

We step off of the small platform, my legs shaky enough that I'm grateful for Madden's strong arm holding me up. A few of the reporters begin to ask questions about how we met and what Madden's platforms will be. He answers all of their questions without hesitation, oozing that confident charm I'm so envious of.

I'm still lost in my haze. Maybe I was stupid to think I could be a politician's wife, fake or not.

⌐≈

Thursday morning, I stop at my parents' new duplex for breakfast. As I walk inside, I smell Mom's cinnamon rolls and freshly brewed coffee. I close the door behind me and fill my lungs with tantalizing scents.

Dad must have heard the door close because he appears at the end of the hallway where the bedrooms are located. I note with a surge of joy that he appears to have graduated from his walker to a cane. He's been working hard with his therapists and the work is definitely paying off.

"Good morning, sweetheart. You're just in time for cinnamon rolls. Mom put them in the oven before she left." Dad walks toward me and pulls me into a hug.

"Look at you, walking around like a pro! I can tell your new PT is working wonders."

He rolls his eyes at my praise. "You act like I haven't been walking perfectly fine for the last 74 years of my life."

I chuckle. "Good point. Where's Mom this morning?"

"She went to her early morning gardening class. Pretty sure she's already friends with everyone who lives here." He laughs.

It warms my heart to see my parents acclimating to their new home so well. I can't deny my overwhelming relief that they're taken care of, and knowing that Madden had a hand in that does funny things to my heart. But maybe that's just indigestion. I certainly hope so, because developing feelings for a man I only married for money would be cumbersome.

I need to remember that Madden didn't pay for my parents' assisted living because he's in love with me; he paid for it as part of our arrangement. And I have my part to play in exchange.

After spending the morning with my dad, I meet up with the girls for lunch and shopping. Since Sophie and Madden are close, I'm hoping she'll tell me what kind of wardrobe might be complementary to his.

We meet at a brick-oven pizza place in the shopping center. Kate is wearing one of her outlandish dresses, of course; this one has cats all over it. I have no clue how she makes these wacky dresses look cute, but somehow she does.

Kate and Sophie spot me walking toward their table and stand to greet me. "There's the new Mrs. Windell!" Kate exclaims as she looks me up and down, taking in my distressed skinny jeans and grey long-sleeve. "Thank goodness you came to us for help. You clearly need our superior fashion advice. You brought Madden's credit card, right?"

"Hey! I just came from my parent's place, not a formal event. Plus, not all of us have purr-fect wardrobes." I make a show of thoroughly looking over her cat dress.

Sophie laughs, spewing some water out of her mouth. "Well played, Odette."

We chat about our week over pizza, and once we've finished up, we clear off the table and amble around to the different shops. The three of us enter a cute little store filled with unique women's clothing, and Kate runs off toward a very colorful display.

"How are things going?" Sophie leans in and asks quietly.

"They're going fine. Besides the few events I attended with him this week, we've hardly seen each other." I shrug. "There's nothing on the schedule for tonight, though, so he said we could spend some time together. Maybe that's a step toward us being friends?"

"Gosh, what an awkward situation. It's gotta be weird living with someone you hardly know." She cringes. "And my brother has a hard time multitasking, so that's great that he chiseled time out to get to know you."

"Hopefully becoming better friends will help with the awkwardness." I sigh. "It's so nice to talk to you about this. You're basically the only person I can confide in besides Madden. I'm bummed that you're leaving tomorrow. We were just starting to get to know each other."

She looks up from rifling through a display of cardigans. "I know. It would be nice to live closer, but I also love being with my military-spouse friends. Their husbands are deployed with Sam, so we hang out all the time."

"Sounds like you have a great support system there. How is your husband doing? Do you get to talk much?"

Her eyes look a little misty. "I think he's doing okay. He's working in a really remote area near Kandahar, so we only get to talk on the phone like once a week. The rest is just email."

"That must be so difficult. And here I am whining about my awkward fake marriage."

Sophie laughs softly. "Hey, my problems don't make yours any less difficult."

We turn as we hear Kate coming up behind us with her arms full of insanely bright patterned clothing. "Are you ready to try things on, Odette?"

Sophie and Kate push me towards the dressing room and, despite my hesitation over Kate's choices, I end up purchasing several items. Who would've thought that adding some color to my wardrobe isn't so scary after all?

Thanks to Sophie and Kate's help, I take home several fashionable yet professional outfits as well as a sleek, black cocktail dress and a formal gown that the girls basically forced me into. The dress is long, mermaid style, and off-the-shoulder with a sweetheart neckline, and the silky fabric is a deep violet color. It even came with a little rhinestone belt. I have no idea what occasion I'll have to wear it, but the girls were extremely convincing.

We say our goodbyes and give Sophie hugs since she leaves tomorrow.

⋘

A little after seven o'clock, I arrive back at the apartment, eager to show Madden my purchases. As the elevator goes up, I think about how surprised he'll be to see my new wardrobe. The man has style and always looks so put together, so he'll probably appreciate the effort I'm putting into looking the part.

Aside from that, I have to admit that I'm looking forward to our evening together. I enjoy spending time with him. Too much, perhaps.

I waltz in the front door, expecting to find Madden relaxing on the couch. But much to my surprise, our apartment is scattered with fliers, pizza boxes, and about a dozen people. Madden and David are the only ones I recognize. I attempt to retreat inside myself to my peaceful space, but it's not working because everyone has looked up to stare at me.

"Odette! How was your day?" Madden walks around the chaos to greet me at the door.

Observing my facial expression, he freezes and smacks his palm to his forehead with a groan. "I completely forgot about tonight. I am so sorry."

I can barely see anymore because of the tears filling my eyes. Everyone seems to be working on the fliers, but I swear I can feel them watching us out of the corner of their eyes. I try my best to choke back the tears and smile in the vicinity of all the blurry blobs currently in my living room.

"Hey, David and... everyone! I'm Odette. It's a pleasure to meet the dream team." I muster up the best smile I can give and then dash down the hallway to my room.

Madden follows me and puts his foot in the doorway to keep me from closing it. "Wait, Odette, please. Come join us. We were just printing fliers and putting together yard signs."

"That's okay. I'm pretty tired. I think I'll just head to bed." I do my best to ignore his handsome, pleading face.

He tries to say something else, but I shut the door before I can hear what it is. Alone in my room, I collapse on the bed in tears, finally allowing the disappointment to wash over me.

⊱─≾

Madden

I feel like the world's biggest jerk as I head back out to the living room. David gives me a skeptical look, but the rest of the team seems oblivious to my marital woes as they continue working on the signs.

David comes into the kitchen and whispers, "What was that all about?"

I rub the back of my neck and sigh. "Odette and I have hardly seen each other all week, so I told her that we could hang out tonight, just the two of us. Obviously, I forgot."

"Dang, Madden. That's pretty bad." He grimaces.

"Thank you, Captain Obvious." I slug him in the shoulder. "I already know I was an idiot, okay? What I don't know is how to make it better."

David shrugs his shoulders. "Don't look at me. I've never even had a serious girlfriend."

"Probably because you end all of your text messages with 'Calc-u-later.'" I cross my arms and give him a knowing look.

"Shut up. Mom says that chicks dig CPAs." He smirks. "And at least I didn't forget my own wife five days after I married her."

I shake my head. "This is all new to me. I'm still learning here. Obviously, though, I'm way out of my depth."

David pushes past me. "Get back to work. I refuse to stay a minute past ten."

Over the next few hours, we finish up the signs to deliver to my supporters this weekend. I was distracted the entire time, knowing I upset Odette, but I couldn't abandon my team and make them do all the work themselves.

After everyone leaves, I walk to her door and gently knock. She doesn't answer, but my knock gently pushes the door slightly ajar. I step inside.

I'm hoping she's awake so we can talk, but as I step further inside the dark room, I see that she is fast asleep on top of the covers, still in her clothes and surrounded by tissues. My heart clenches.

I did this to her. I made her cry herself to sleep.

This is a disaster. I haven't even been married for an entire week and I'm already screwing this up. Feeling angry with myself, I ball my hands into fists. I always become so focused on work that I'm blind to everything else around me. I know it's a weakness of mine, but it didn't really matter until now. My dad was always a work-a-holic too; maybe that's one reason why he and Mom aren't happy.

This is probably why Jen ended up with Bryan. He was actually there for her. For the first time, it hits me that Jen probably didn't hate the idea of me being a politician as much as she hated how I always put my aspirations first, even above her. Odette didn't marry me for love, but I definitely don't want her to be miserable.

Out of the corner of my eye, I spot a fluffy blanket folded at the end of the bed. I gently pull it up over Odette's sleeping figure and then quietly creep out of the room, closing the door behind me.

Once I'm in bed, I try to think of a way to fix things and come up with nothing. This must be why most newlyweds go on honeymoons: so they don't spend their first weeks of marriage bickering.

The next morning I shower and get dressed quickly, then start planning my apology to my wife. I can smell fresh coffee from the hallway, so I expect to see her when I walk into the kitchen. But to my surprise, she's not in the kitchen, dining room or living area. Nervousness takes root, and my stomach drops. *Did she leave?*

I check my phone and see a missed text from her.

Odette: Left early this morning so I could have breakfast with my parents. I left some coffee for you. See you tonight.

My shoulders relax and I let out a sigh of relief as I type out my response.

Me: Thanks for the coffee. I'm sorry again about last night. Raincheck for Sunday?

If I had more time, I would drive straight to her parent's place and talk to her in person. I'm supposed to meet my campaign team in less than an hour, though, to dispense the signs and fliers we finished putting together last night.

Balancing a congressional campaign and a new wife is so much more complicated than I had expected.

Chapter 16

Odette

My dad's nurse usually comes in the morning at nine o'clock, so I arrive promptly at eight to get an entire hour of alone time with my parents. My early arrival definitely has nothing to do with avoiding my husband, of course.

It's cathartic to sit here with my parents, eating breakfast and chatting–just what my heart needs. They look content here in their little duplex. But my parents have always been that sweet couple you see holding hands and doting on each other. They never had much money, but it didn't matter because they truly loved each other. I sigh and take a sip of my coffee.

The mature adult deep down inside of me knows that I need to move past my irritation with Madden. I definitely don't want to be one of those whiny, high-maintenance wives. But I can't shake my hurt from the night before. I don't expect romance, of course, but I hoped for friendship at least.

I'm so deep in thought that I don't hear Mom calling my name until she waves her hand in front of my face. "Odette? Earth to Odette."

I glance at her over the rim of my coffee mug. "Oh, sorry, Mom. I must need more coffee."

Dad regards me curiously. "What's going on in that mind of yours?"

I hesitate for a moment, contemplating how to answer honestly without giving too many details. My parents still think Madden and I married for love, much to my eternal guilt "It's just... Madden is so busy with the campaign, and I truly understand that. But we had one evening we could have spent together, and he forgot all about it."

Mom pats the top of my hand. "Oh, hon, I'm sorry. I can't even imagine starting out a marriage while also campaigning."

"You two will definitely have to face some unique challenges this year. Try to be patient with him," Dad says gently.

"I know. I'm frustrated with myself for feeling upset about it. I think I'm just annoyed because I had been looking forward to a quiet evening together. He obviously didn't care as much." I shrug one shoulder.

"Well, the only thing you can do is communicate how you feel, even though you probably don't feel like it. Behind every splendid marriage is an exhausting amount of communication. Believe me." Mom gives Dad a wink from across the table.

"It's true." Dad chuckles. "I can't count the times that Mom was angry with me and I didn't know until she really spelled it out. Where is Madden today, anyway?"

"He's with his team, handing out fliers and delivering yard signs to supporters." I rest my chin in my hands.

Mom places her hand on my shoulder. "Odette, you know your father and I are always here to listen, but your husband is the one you should talk to. And if you want to spend time with him, jumping in with his campaign team might be just the way to do that."

I look down at my feet, feeling ashamed for lying to them. Here they are giving me sincere, loving advice, when they don't even know the reality of the situation. Slowly, I look back up, hoping my face doesn't betray the shame I'm trying so desperately to hide. "You guys are right. I do need to talk to him."

Dad grins. "Gotta rip off the band-aid, baby girl."

When Dad's nurse arrives, I hug my parents goodbye and send Madden a text asking where they are. He responds quickly with a Google Maps link.

Our marriage might not be typical, but we still have to live with each other and get along. So, hesitantly, I plug his location into my GPS and start driving that direction.

⟵⥺

Madden

Odette didn't explain why she wanted my location. I wonder if I should be nervous. She might drive by and egg all of my signs.

David and I map out our route as we walk. I want to get as many fliers out and talk with as many voters as we can. I want people to see that I truly care, that I want to have genuine conversations, which is why I'm out here doing the grunt work with my entire campaign team.

Suddenly, I hear a soft voice behind us. "Madden, David! Wait up." We look over our shoulders and see Odette walking towards us.

David raises his eyebrows. "I'm guessing you two patched things up?"

"Not yet. I tried to talk to her last night, but she was already asleep."

"You mean to tell me that you did nothing to appease your wife, and yet here she is with a smile on her face?"

I give him a teasing jab to the ribs. "Apparently. She's clearly too good for me."

He pats me on the back. "I think she's the magical unicorn of women. Keep her around."

I wiggle my ring finger, flashing the titanium wedding band at him. "Don't really have a choice, not that I mind."

Odette finally catches up to us and wrings her hands together. "Hey! I thought I'd join the team today. Is that okay?"

A wide grin spreads across my face. "Of course! You'll love working with the dream team."

David walks ahead of us. Without thinking, I reach over and pull Odette's hand into mine. She looks up at me, eyes wide, then quickly drops her gaze to her feet. I hope I'm not making her uncomfortable. Public PDA is in the contract, though, which is the only reason I'm holding her hand, of course.

Now that we have a moment alone together, we need to talk about what happened last night. "Odette, I know that I hurt you last night and I'm so sorry."

"It's fine. You already apologized." She attempts to smile, but I can tell that she's still hurt.

"No, it's not. I'm sorry I forgot about our plans. When I'm focused on a task, I tend to ignore everyone around me." I rub my thumb on the back of her hand. "Obviously, I need to consider you when making plans."

She shrugs her shoulders. "We're both still figuring this out. And spending quality time isn't in the contract. But I do appreciate the apology." She gives me a real smile this time.

"It may not be in the contract, but since we're married, we might as well be friends, right?"

"I'd like that."

I grin. "How about we do an early morning coffee date every week? We both get up early anyway, and if there's one thing I know, it's that we both love coffee."

She looks into my eyes, holding my gaze. "I would love that, really."

I give her hand a squeeze. "It's a date."

"It's a date," she replies with an adorable blush.

Chapter 17

Odette

♥

Two weeks later, Kansas Day rolls around—the day we celebrate Kansas becoming a state. Naturally, it's a pretty big deal in Kansas. Even aside from that, I've been looking forward to it all month because Madden and I are spending the day together at an elementary school an hour away. As Wichita isn't the only city in the fourth district, it's important for Madden to make appearances in other cities as well. And, since education is one of his main platforms, today we're dressing up like pioneers and reading books about our state to several classrooms of children.

We rented historically accurate costumes from a local costume shop to make it more fun for the kids. Unfortunately, the shop failed to inform me that my period-correct frock has about fifty buttons to fasten in the back. I stare in dismay at my reflection in my bedroom mirror, twisting to inspect the row of gaping buttons running down my back.

Heat rushes to my face. Unless I want to scandalize a pack of children, I have no choice but to ask Madden for help.

As if he can read my mind, Madden knocks on my bedroom door. When I open it, he swaggers into the room with a grin, wearing trousers, a buttoned-up vest, and a matching jacket.

I take in his ensemble from head-to-toe and *wow*. He can hitch his horses to my covered wagon any day. It's annoyingly obvious that this man would be handsome in any decade.

"Milady," he bows. "You look beautiful." He nods at my dress appreciatively.

I sigh and look down. There's no way I look as good as he does. My skirt and waistcoat are navy blue satin with off-white velvet trim, and the waistcoat is lined with gold buttons in the front. I'm sure the settlers back in 1877 didn't dress this fancy, but it's fun to pretend.

I curtsy. "You look pretty handsome yourself."

"Are you ready to take to the carriage?" Madden flashes me a boyish smile.

"Actually, I need your help." I turn slightly to show him my predicament.

His Adam's apple bobs as he swallows. "Okay, sure. Turn around." He twirls his index finger, motioning me to spin.

As his hands fumble nervously with the buttons, his breathing deepens. Maybe he has a cold or something. The feel of his warm hands drifting their way up my spine, securing each button, is pure torture. I'm most likely blushing from head to toe because the room suddenly feels boiling hot.

I must be losing my mind. Kansas Day is not sensual. I just need to pretend to be a tough pioneer woman and get my hormones under control.

Fifty buttons and one uncomfortable hour later, we finally arrive at the school in Madden's Audi, sitting in our crinkly 19th-century clothing. I jump out to adjust my bustle and get the yards of fabric under control.

The principal greets us and gives us a quick tour of the school, leading us to the first class Madden will read to. As we enter, I see that a local news station is already set up in the back of the room. The crew waves to us quietly.

This is the type of attention politicians love. Madden has been talking about reading to these kids for weeks, though, so I know he's genuinely excited. I'm positive he would gladly do this even without media coverage.

Madden takes his seat in front of twenty-four adorable, rambunctious kindergarteners and animatedly chats with them about our state. One little girl tells him all about the Kansas state bird, the Meadowlark. Then a boy with freckles shows him a picture he painted of a sunflower. Eventually, everyone quiets down and Madden reads a children's book to them, explaining how Kansas came to be a state. He patiently answers questions as the kids raise their hands excitedly.

A smile creeps onto my face. He is a natural. I almost can't handle the cuteness. My ovaries are about to jump out of my body, drag Madden into a janitor's closet, and demand a baby from him.

What is with me today? Who knew that a man dressed in 1870s garb would be such a turn-on for me?

We circuit through the various classrooms–the news crew following silently–and interact with the kids. Madden even takes his lunch break with them. By the end of the day, we're both exhausted and I'm ready to get home and change into some sweats. Despite my tiredness, today was incredible. Honestly, it was the most fun that I've had in a long time.

⋐

Three weeks after our Kansas day escapade, we're downtown at a chic little coffee shop called The Bean. Our weekly coffee dates have really helped us get to know each other and I find myself looking forward to them each Wednesday.

"How are your parents doing?" Madden takes a sip of his steaming hot coffee. "Sorry I haven't made it over to their house in weeks."

"That's okay. They understand that you're busy." I shrug. "My birthday is next week, though. They were hoping we might come over for dinner to celebrate."

He smacks his palm to his forehead. "I never even asked when your birthday was."

I laugh. "To be fair, I don't know your birthday, either. Mine is Friday, by the way–February 23rd."

He pulls out his phone and types it into his calendar. "Good to know. Mine is March 20th. So you're a month older than me." He bites his bottom lip to hold back a smile.

I cock my head to the side. "What's so funny about that?"

"It's just... well, you're kind of a cougar." He tries unsuccessfully to contain his laughter.

"Oh, stop! *One* month doesn't make me a cougar. And if I remember correctly, you were the one who *begged* me to marry you."

His mouth opens in mock horror. "Your comebacks are so savage sometimes. But, to answer your question, I'm free to come to dinner Friday."

"Thank you. My parents will be thrilled."

"Now I just need to think of the perfect present." He brings his hand to his chin and makes a show of pondering about it.

I shake my head from side to side. "Oh, no you don't. No presents."

"Come on! You're not one of those low-maintenance girls who hates presents, are you?" He feigns a pained expression.

"If you must get me a present, you can get me a Pomeranian puppy."

His smile disappears. "Don't you dare even joke about that."

⤜⚘

On Friday, Madden walks me out to the parking lot so we can drive to my parents' house. He has had a strange grin on his face for the last hour and I'm getting very suspicious as to why. But then I spot it in the slot next to his Audi: a shiny white car with an oversized, pink bow on top.

My eyes fly wide open. "Where's my Buick?"

"I replaced it. Happy birthday!" Madden beams.

"You did not buy me a car. Madden, this is way too much!" I shake my head.

He shrugs. "It's just a Honda Civic. No big deal."

"It's a brand new car! What am I supposed to do with it two years from now?"

"The car is already paid for. You can keep it. And, honestly, you driving a Buick while I'm speeding around in my Audi kind of made me look like a crappy husband."

I scowl at him. "My Pomeranian better be in there."

He briefly scowls at my comment then unlocks the Civic, obviously excited to show me all the bells and whistles. Madden tosses me the keys with a big grin and I drive my new car to my parent's place.

I'm still a bit uncomfortable with the gift but not enough to reject it. Not gonna lie: connecting my phone to Bluetooth will be incredibly handy.

I park in front of my parents' duplex. I have to hide my grin when Mom opens the door before we even knock. She's *that* excited to have us both for dinner that she must have stood watch by the window for our arrival. She and Dad crowd the doorway with big smiles on their faces.

"Happy 29th!" They exclaim. Mom sets a plastic tiara on top of my head before I'm through the doorway. Looking over our shoulders, she spots the car. "Is that new?"

"I replaced the Buick for her birthday. I hope that's okay." Madden says with a smile.

"Doesn't bother me," Dad says. "'Bout time."

"I am just happy that you take such good care of Odette." My mom's eyes are filled with tears. Madden flinches slightly at her remark. But I don't think my parents notice.

Guilt suddenly makes my stomach churn. My parents will be devastated when we end our marriage. Closing my eyes for a second, I try to push the thought away and just focus on enjoying the evening. We'll worry about that when it comes.

Mom made my favorite meal: BBQ meatballs, baked potatoes, and a birthday cake, of course. They even got me a few small gifts.

The evening runs smoothly until they start sharing my embarrassing childhood stories with Madden. I groan and cover my face with my hands when they recount my nature-loving phase. I used to collect plant samples to grow on my windowsill, though they all died within days. I even painstakingly created a t-shirt emblazoned with "1-800-NatureGirl" and wore it around almost daily.

But as we all laugh together throughout the evening, it hits me again just how hard it will be–not only on me, but on my family– when my contract with Madden ends. Would it be more merciful to just tell my parents now?

I immediately dismiss the thought. It would surely hurt them more if my parents knew that I married a stranger to pay for their care. I'll learn to live with this guilt in my gut.

I have to.

Chapter 18

Madden

♥

We have a free evening the day after Odette's birthday, an uncommon occurrence these days. I usually thrive with busyness, constantly having something to do and somewhere to go, but lately, I find myself more and more content to stay home with Odette and enjoy peaceful evenings together.

She's waiting for me on the couch with a smorgasbord of Chinese takeout spread across the coffee table. I join her with two orange-flavored Fantas, flick on the TV, and take my seat next to her.

The news blares to life on the screen. I'm about to change the channel when something familiar catches my eye. I squint to make sure I'm seeing straight, then throw back my head with a dramatic groan. "Christopher Highman?"

"Who's that?"

"He's the jerk I used to have the displeasure of working with. You met him briefly when we signed the prenup. And the chubby, bald guy standing in front is his dad, Larry. I used to see him coming out of Christopher's office every so often."

We both focus our attention on the TV. Larry Highman and his wife, along with their three adult children, walk onto a small stage adorned with a Kansas flag and an American flag.

Odette grimaces. "It looks like they're making an announcement."

"Oh, no," I whisper. I know what's happening.

Larry Highman steps up to a microphone on screen. The camera cuts to a close-up of his face. "Thank you for joining us this evening. My family and I are extremely excited to announce my candidacy for the fourth district congressional race. I look forward to representing our great state of Kansas!" The on-screen crowd erupts in cheers.

Odette and I stare blankly at the screen.

I turn the TV off. I can't stare at my old coworker and his family any longer. "This is bad. So far, the only person running against me is a Democrat named Mark Jones, and I'm not too worried about him. But Larry Highman could be a real threat. He'll have the Republican vote in his pocket right from the start." I scrub my hands down my face.

"Do you know anything about him?" Odette asks innocently.

"I've only met Larry a few times. Aside from being filthy rich and raising a jerk son, I honestly don't know what he's like."

Odette stands up and walks across the room to grab her laptop. "Alright, so let's find dirt on this Larry guy." She says his name like it's laced with poison, and I love her for it. Well, not *love*, per se.

"Good plan. We need to be prepared. If he's anything like his son, he may play dirty during this election." She returns to the couch, laptop in hand. I scoot closer to look over her shoulder so I can see the computer screen. I could go get my own laptop, but Odette smells nice, and this is the perfect excuse to sit close to her.

"Looks like our evening just filled up." She looks up at me, our noses almost touching. Her breath hitches and she looks away quickly, worrying her bottom lip. "I guess we need to be extra convincing now, huh?"

I smirk. "Really? How so?"

Her cheeks turn bright red as she stumbles over her words. "I mean, I just meant... Christopher saw us in Bennington's office."

I chuckle at her embarrassment, then sober at the realization. "Don't worry about Christopher. I'm sure he didn't think anything of our meeting with Richard. When Christopher gets married, he'll probably sign a prenup as well."

"Right. I forgot that he's rich, too," she mutters.

"How about we finish dinner first and *then* you can help me research Larry?"

She nods excitedly and scoops up some chicken fried rice.

⌁

Saturday rolls around and we haven't found much useful info on Larry Highman throughout the week. All we know is that he owns an investment firm and some real estate, including a few apartment complexes in town. It's hardly enough to build a campaign strategy with.

Today Odette and I are getting primped for a photoshoot for the Washington Journal. They're doing an article on me since I'm the youngest person running for Congress this year. It should be great publicity, and it will give me new photos to use for my website.

The hair and make-up crew have taken over our apartment. There's a make-up lady with something resembling a tool belt of brushes buckled around her waist, a hair guy, and another man who just seems to float around assisting where needed. They've seated Odette and I next to each other at the dining table, which I can't even see anymore through all of the bottles and brushes covering it. Before today, I had no idea that this many hair and makeup products existed. I'm unsure why they even felt the need to cover Odette's already perfect face with all of that... stuff.

I glance at Odette in the chair next to me, her eyes closed as the make-up lady smooths something across her eyelids. I assume that this photoshoot won't be Odette's favorite activity. When we're at campaign events, she tends to carry herself very modestly and stay in the background, though for the life of me I can't figure out why she hates being in the spotlight. A woman that beautiful should have every reason to feel confident. Instead, she seems to be wracked by self-consciousness.

Just as I'm about to ask if they're almost finished, my sister's face pops up on my phone, requesting FaceTime.

I slide the bar to answer. "Hey, sis!"

"Madden!" Sophie beams. "Is Odette there, too?"

"We're both here!" I lean the phone to the right so she can see us both. Odette tries to smile at Sophie, but the make-up artist fusses at her to keep still. "Getting ready for some fancy photos. How was your appointment?"

"Amazing! Your little *niece* looks perfect and healthy!"

Odette squeals. "A baby girl! That's so exciting! Congrats!"

"Mom is going to spoil her rotten, and so will all of her uncles," I warn.

Sophie just laughs. "I know. It's going to be ridiculous. Odette, will you tell Kate for me?"

"Of course. What was your husband's reaction?"

"Sam is over the moon! This deployment has been especially difficult for him, so it was nice to give him some good news." She smiles, but I see a touch of worry in her eyes. "Well, I have to let you go so I can tell the rest of the family!"

"Alright, love you."

"Bye, Sophie!" Odette gives a little wave to the screen.

I hang up the phone. The make-up artist gives Odette a final dusting of something or other, sprays her hair with a can resembling bug spray (although I'm hoping that's not what it is), then removes her cape.

The hair and makeup team quickly scurries about the room, packing away their make-shift beauty salon. The clean-up takes astronomically less time than set-up. Within a few minutes, they've gathered up their mess and headed out the door. I hardly notice, though. Everything happening in the background fades as my eyes drift over my wife.

I take in her beauty from her shiny red hair, plump red lips, white button-up shirt tucked into high-waisted black trousers, and pointy patent-leather pumps. Apparently, Odette in business casual makes me weak in the knees.

She blinks her luminous green eyes at me. "Do I look okay?"

"You look more than okay. You look amazing. Is this how you dressed for work in D.C.? How on earth did you stay single?"

Her face falls. I've hit a nerve, apparently. "Well, I... I think I was just too boring. No one I went on a date with bothered to ask me out a second time." She shrugs like it's no big deal, but her eyes tell a different story.

"Those men were obviously out of their minds," I scoff. "I'm lucky to have you as my wife."

"Your *fake* wife."

"Real or fake, their loss is my gain."

"Please. Under normal circumstances, you would've never married me." Her eyes nearly bug out of her head like she's surprised that she said those words aloud.

I furrow my brow. "Do you know how many miserable dates I went on trying to find someone I could even tolerate? Then I saw you at Thanksgiving and it just... clicked. You made me feel at ease. Whatever happened in D.C., you're definitely *not* boring."

She averts her eyes shyly and twirls a lock of her hair. "Thank you for saying that."

I grab her hand and grin. "Come on, wife. Time to wow the cameras."

Chapter 19

Odette

♥

P ierce, the Washington Journal photographer, a journalist named Lee, and Paul Newhouse meet us outside The Wichita Museum of Art. There's a beautiful walking path to the side of the building, scattered with asymmetrical sculptures and shaded by large weeping willow trees, with the winding Wichita River serving as a picturesque backdrop. It's no wonder that the photographer wanted to shoot here.

There's a lot of photography equipment, making me feel a little uneasy. This is a much bigger production than I realized. Madden's kind words back at the apartment give me a boost of confidence, though. Whenever he compliments me, I feel warm all over. My brain knows better than to develop feelings for him, but my body doesn't seem to mind the idea.

"Ah, there they are! Odette, you look lovely." Paul walks toward us from the museum steps where he was talking with the two Washington Journal visitors. He wrinkles his nose at Madden. "And I guess you look alright."

"Hey! I thought I was the beauty and she was the brains?" Madden says as he winks at me.

The photographer approaches and interrupts our banter to give us a quick rundown. We'll start with outdoor photos before the sun goes down and then finish up inside the museum. He shoos us to the right of the building where all the photography lighting has been set up in front of a small grove of willow trees. He has a list of specific shots he needs, so he sets out to arrange Madden and I accordingly.

We start out pretty stoic, with me leaning against a tree and Madden putting his arm around my waist as we try to look severe and professional. Then Pierce takes some photos of us walking hand in hand. The photoshoot goes on like this for an hour before we move indoors. The journalist walks beside Madden, asking questions about his childhood and his campaign in between shots.

Then everything takes a turn when the photographer looks through some of the photos on his camera and announces, "We need something sexier."

Madden speaks up quickly. "What exactly do you mean by *sexier*? I'm running for Congress, not *America's Next Top Model*."

"Well, you two just seem a little stiff. Relax, kiss each other, get cozy. You guys are newlyweds. People eat that stuff up." He hunkers down behind his camera.

Paul smirks. "Alright, Madden! Kiss your bride." I can tell that he's biting the inside of his cheeks to keep from laughing.

Madden steps closer to me but hesitates. I wonder if he can hear my heart beating frantically in my chest. He slips both hands around my waist. His eyes lock with mine as he slowly brings our foreheads together.

My surroundings seem to fade as Madden pulls me in tighter. I completely forget about our audience. All I can think about is Madden's gorgeous blue eyes, the warmth of his hands on me, and the sound of my own heart drumming in my ears.

It's all in the contract. This isn't real.

And then he leans the rest of the way in. Our lips meet.

But this isn't a sweet kiss like the one on our wedding day. No, this kiss is urgent and hungry. He pulls back and his eyes look dark, darker than I've ever seen them. Then he kisses me again.

Without thinking, my hands grab onto the lapels of his suit jacket to bring him closer. His fingers find their way into my hair, making goosebumps break out all over my body. He's probably making my hair a mess, but I don't care.

I don't know how long we stand there kissing, but eventually, the photographer clears his throat. "Okay, thanks, guys. I, um, got several good shots. We're good."

Madden and I disentangle ourselves a little awkwardly. I step back to put some distance between us. Paul just stares at us with an extremely amused expression on his face.

Madden's face reddens, which is refreshing because usually, it's only *my* face that does that. I feel conflicted. I mean, sure, that kiss was incredible. It may even have been the best kiss of my life. Okay, it was definitely the best kiss of my life.

How am I supposed to keep my feelings out of this when he kisses me like that?

⋖⋅ℰ

Madden

After the photoshoot, I head straight back to the apartment to take a very cold shower. I cannot believe I let myself get so carried away with that kiss. It just felt so good in the moment. It's like her lips pulled me into another dimension and I lost all sense of reality.

I cannot lose control like that again, for Odette's sake as well as mine. I have to keep my feelings in check. Odette and I have become friends, and I'm comfortable with our relationship. If we can keep it that way, this marriage won't get any more complicated than it already is.

Did I like kissing her? Obviously. Would I mind sharing a bedroom with her? Definitely not.

But that's not the purpose of our arrangement.

Once I'm thoroughly cooled off, I throw on some basketball shorts and a casual v-neck and walk back out to the living room. Odette is sitting on the sofa, still in her dress clothes.

She looks up at me, her mouth twisted like she's not sure whether she wants to say what's on her mind or not. After a few seconds, she starts. "So... that was a very... convincing kiss."

I run both hands through my wet hair. "Sorry about that... I hope I didn't make you uncomfortable."

She looks down at her hands folded neatly in her lap. "Don't apologize. I mean, millions of Washington Journal readers will see the photos, so we needed to be convincing, right? And PDA is in the contract, after all." She looks up and meets my gaze.

"Right. We *needed* to be convincing. For the public."

Odette rises, still looking a little uncomfortable, and slowly walks back to her bedroom.

I stop myself from following her. There's nothing I can say to ease the awkwardness. I crossed a line today and I can't let myself do that again. It wouldn't be fair to Odette.

Even if it's not real, I can't bear the idea of having a miserable marriage like my own parents, which is exactly what would happen if we let our feelings get involved. She would quickly realize how career-focused I am and see that I can't offer her the love and attention she deserves. Jen discovered that about me, just like my mom discovered that about my father.

Deep down, I think what truly scares me is that I can actually picture myself caring less about my goals and more about making Odette happy. And after everything I've sacrificed for my congressional dreams, that's simply not an option.

⊰⊱

Over the next two weeks, I put some space between Odette and myself. She seems tense around me. I thought we had resolved things when we talked about the kiss and both agreed that it was part of the contract, but still, our conversations are stilted and her answers to my questions are short and clipped. At least she has continued helping me with campaign tasks and showing up for events. Hopefully, once Odette sees that I can control myself, the tension will fade and we can go back to the friendly, casual relationship we've enjoyed thus far.

Tonight I have the opportunity to speak at a charity for immigrants, which is a welcome distraction from the tension between Odette and I. Odette even helped me write my speech, which was the most time we have spent together since our photoshoot make-out session.

The immigration charity banquet is at a beautiful catholic church in town, where the organizers clearly went all-out with tonight's event. The tables are draped in white linen and feature beautiful ceramic centerpieces made by local immigrants. They're even available for purchase, and all the proceeds go to charity.

As I walk onto the stage to give my speech, I see the crowd of people seated at their circular tables in the large banquet room, their eyes fixed on me. But it's not their eyes I'm looking for. I find Odette in the crowd, her twinkling emerald eyes drawing me in for a few seconds. It reminds me of when our eyes locked at our high school reunion so many months ago.

I blink a few times to refocus, then step up to the mic. "Thank you all so much for welcoming my wife and I here tonight. It's an honor to speak on a topic so close to my heart."

I begin my speech by sharing my grandparent's story. Then I roll into the part Odette wrote with me.

"My great-great-grandparents were just two of many immigrants from around the world who came to the United States. Our immigrants set our country apart from others. With their unique experience, they have shaped our culture and enriched our American entrepreneurial spirit.

However, our immigration system is flawed. As your congressman, I plan to introduce a bill that will not only make American borders more secure but will also issue proper documentation to undocumented immigrants currently residing in the United States. This would secure their ability to gain citizenship *and* allow them to stay in our great country along with their families.

Streamlining the citizenship process for our immigrants will help our economy as well as encourage others to come into our country legally. We cannot survive without the indomitable strength and pioneering gifts of immigrants. Thank you very much."

The crowd stands and applauds. I can't help but look at Odette with a grin as I exit the stage. Several people come to shake my hand afterward and Odette joins me at the front of the room. Together we continue shaking hands and mingling with everyone.

An hour later we're about to leave just as Leonard and Emma Johnson, the organization's founders, stop us.

"What a fantastic speech! Thank you so much for being our guest speaker this evening," Mrs. Johnson says as she shakes my hand, then turns her attention toward Odette. "And you must be Mrs. Windell."

Odette smiles graciously as she loops her arm through mine. "Yes. I have the honor of standing by Madden's side through his campaign. I can confirm how passionate he is about this cause."

"Oh, I could tell just by his heartfelt speech!" Mrs. Johnson beams.

"Hearing him talk about his great-great-grandparents was just one of the things that made me fall in love with him." Odette bats her lashes at me.

To anyone who doesn't know her, she's simply oozing with charm as she dotes on me. But I hear the sarcasm and see the angry twinkle in her eyes. Our stupid, wonderful, idiotic, amazing kiss has apparently taken us from friends to co-workers.

No, that's not right. The kiss didn't; *I* did.

On our way home from the charity banquet, Odette is deathly quiet.

"Those were quite the praises you sang about me to Mrs. Johnson," I say when I can't take the silence anymore.

"Oh, you know me. I love a good opportunity to brag about you," she responds dryly and continues looking out the window.

"Odette, I know that you're upset with me and we need to talk about it."

"Did you expect me *not* to be upset when you practically made out with me and then ignored me for two weeks?"

"Alright, I deserve that." I take a deep breath. "Obviously, I enjoyed kissing you–a little too much, in fact. So, I tried to put some distance between us. I thought that maybe we were getting too close."

She finally looks at me from the passenger seat. I'm driving, but I look over at her just long enough to see the hurt in her eyes. "But why? We're going to have to kiss each other again, eventually. And I enjoy spending time with you. So why can't we continue being friends?"

"Of course we can be friends. But... we'll only be married for a few years. I mean, what if we developed feelings for each other? I'd never be able to make you happy. In past relationships, I was too focused on work to give the love and attention my partners needed," I say, thinking about Jen. "I don't want to repeat history. It's probably safer if we keep some distance between us."

"You don't think we can be friends without wanting more?" Her voice sounds shaky.

I pin her with a serious look. "Odette, I couldn't even kiss you for a photoshoot without it getting out of hand."

"Okay, fair point." She blushes and bites her bottom lip.

I look away. I can't see her do that and *not* think about kissing her. "So let's just stick to the contract and give each other some space, okay?"

"Alright."

Chapter 20

Odette

♥

“ Aren't you glad we talked you into getting this gorgeous dress?”

Kate says as she finishes the last touches on my makeup from her bathroom, which she has magically transformed into a makeshift beauty salon.

Two days after the immigration banquet, we already have another big event to attend. Tonight is the Wichita Fine Arts Society's annual gala. Everyone who's anyone in Wichita will be there, meaning there will be lots of influential people and many deep pockets. It's important that we convince the public that Madden and I are a real couple, especially since a Republican is now running against him for the fourth district.

According to Paul's research, Larry Highman automatically looks like the better option because he's 60-years-old, has been married for 30 years, and has three grown children. Tonight's gala is the perfect place to gain new supporters and rub elbows with important business owners in the city, so Larry will undoubtedly attend with his wife.

As I attach the rhinestone belt to my violet mermaid-style gown, I take in my reflection. Kate swept my hair back in a sleek chignon and played up the drama of my makeup with smokey eyeshadow, long dark lashes, and glossy nude lips. “Wow, Kate. You missed your calling as a make-up artist. I look... beautiful.”

She hugs my shoulders from behind. “Of course you do, because you *are* beautiful! There's no way Madden can keep his hands off of you tonight." She winks at me in the mirror.

I chuckle awkwardly. "Right. I'm just excited about the delicious food and dancing."

"I wish I could come with you. We could burn up the dance floor all night." Kate breaks out into the macarena.

I laugh. "I'm pretty sure this gala is way too fancy-schmancy for the macarena."

"Darn. I hope they chose a good caterer, at least." Kate gives my hair one last mist of hairspray.

My phone pings with a text from Madden. "Looks like we finished up just in time. Madden is here to pick me up." I give Kate a quick hug. "Thanks again for making me look presentable!"

"Of course! Have some fun and get that husband of yours to bust a few moves on the dance floor!" Kate says as she air-kisses my cheeks. I grab my clutch and fur wrap, then give her a brief wave as I head out the door of her house.

I doubt I could get Madden to hold my hand tonight, let alone dance. Our relationship isn't as amicable and light-hearted as it was before our kiss. What he said about keeping our distance made sense, but part of me wonders what's so wrong about us being attracted to each other. What if this marriage actually became more than just a business arrangement? Couldn't that be a good thing?

I feel a little sorry for him that he believes he could never make a good husband. Jen really did a number on the poor guy.

Pulling the door closed behind me, I turn and find Madden leaning against his Audi in the driveway. My jaw nearly drops at the sight of him. He's wearing a black tuxedo complete with a black satin bowtie and matching cumberbund.

I hear someone say, "Wow, you look incredibly handsome." Heat rushes to my cheeks when I realize *I'm* the one that said it. It just tumbled out of me before I could stop it.

"Thanks." He shrugs awkwardly. "You look beautiful, too. I mean, not that you said I was beautiful... but you are." He clears his throat, then quickly glances at my dress and back up to my face.

"Thanks," I say with a smirk, a bit amused, since he's usually so suave and confident. I gather my skirt into one hand and descend the porch steps. He meets me at the passenger side of the car. "I know you'll be busy tonight, but do you think you could make time for just one dance?"

"Of course." He opens the car door for me.

We drive across town to the large City Arts building. It's one of the more modern buildings in Wichita, covered in glass windows and surrounded by a landscape of interesting, Roman-inspired sculptures. The valet takes our vehicle, and I plaster on my most convincing smile, taking my husband's arm.

As soon as we step inside, I hear the live band playing classical music over the hundreds of people talking. The men are dressed nicely in tuxedos and the ladies are wearing various styles and colors of formal gowns. The room looks like a very expensive rainbow.

Paul and his wife, Marie, sidle up next to us. Paul looks handsome in a black tux and blue tie. His wife wears a long blue dress that matches Paul's tie, and her grey, shoulder-length hair is smoothly swept back with a sparkly clip on one side. He and Marie make a lovely pair, both tall and slim.

We spend a few minutes mingling with those around us. Madden spots a striking couple who must be in their fifties and guides me over to them.

"The man with the mustache is John Darling, and the blonde lady next to him is his wife, Nina. He's CEO of the largest bank in Wichita." He leans down to whisper, his lips briefly brushing against my ear, causing my breath to hitch.

As we draw closer to them, Mr. Darling notices us. "Madden!" He reaches out to shake Madden's hand firmly. "Just played golf with your dad yesterday and he said you'd be here!"

"It's hard to believe my dad makes time to play golf these days." He chuckles.

"Yes, but we all have to slow down, eventually. You'll understand when you're old like us," Mr. Darling says with a wink.

"Let me introduce you to my wife. This is Odette." Madden slips his arm around my waist. I try to focus on the couple in front of us instead of the heat spreading through my entire body at Madden's touch.

Mr. Darling shakes my hand. "Pleasure to meet you! It's about time Madden settled down. Life is better with a good woman by your side." He gives his wife a kiss on the cheek and then introduces her.

Mr. Darling takes a sip of his champagne, then asks, "How's the campaign going?"

"It's going great. I had the privilege of speaking at a charity event for immigrants a few days ago."

Mrs. Darling flags down a cocktail waiter and grabs two glasses of champagne for Madden and I. "Oh, that's wonderful! Immigration is a very important issue to us." As she speaks, I realize she has an accent.

"Nina immigrated here from the Ukraine with her family." Mr. Darling smiles fondly at his wife.

"And thank goodness you did! Dad has said several times that John would be a mess without you," Madden tells Mrs. Darling with a cheeky grin.

I realize suddenly that Madden brought up the immigration charity intentionally, knowing that it would endear him to the Darlings. He knows what he's doing.

"Madden, why don't you come golf with your Dad and I next week? I'd love to discuss supporting your campaign." He cups his hand over his mouth, pretending his wife can't hear. "Mrs. Darling won't let me talk business at these events."

She laughs and playfully hits him on the shoulder.

"Sounds like a plan! Although my golf game is probably rusty," Madden replies.

"Not a problem. I'm more generous when I win, anyway." Mr. Darling raises his champagne glass as he and his wife begin drifting back into the crowd.

As we walk away from the Darlings, I stare up at my husband, who's positively glowing after effortlessly gaining another supporter. I love seeing him in action, winning people over with his genuine kindness.

I groan inwardly. I was kidding myself thinking I could be married to him and not develop feelings. My heart is falling so fast for him. If only he would allow his heart to fall for me, too.

After cocktail hour we all sit down for dinner. Awkwardly, Larry and Barbara Highman are seated at the same table with us, as well as Paul and Marie, and another couple I've never met. Despite Googling Larry last week with Madden, I never would've recognized him in person. His professional photos online were clearly edited for his website. Face to face he's much chubbier than his photos, and even the nearly nonexistent hairline looks more sparse. I don't think he's taken very good care of himself. His wife is also quite plump, but her brown curls, rosy cheeks, and big smile give her a bright, matronly look.

I'm thankful that Paul's wife is here, so I have someone to chat with as the men talk politics. Unsurprisingly, Madden chats easily with Larry about what their campaigns have looked like thus far. It probably helps that they've met before, seeing as Madden worked with his son at the law firm. There's something about Larry that makes me leery, though. Perhaps it's the way he seems to glare lasers at my husband's back anytime Madden looks away.

After the meal, the band strikes a lively tune and a few couples take to the dance floor. I look at Madden, hoping he remembers that he promised me a dance, but he and Paul have more people they'd like to speak with. They wander from the table, leaving Marie and I to chat with two other ladies still sitting at our table.

After an hour, I get anxious and scan the room for Madden. Surely he'll come back, right? He promised me a dance.

Marie places her hand atop mine. "Don't worry, dear. I'm sure he'll be back soon."

"I really hope so. I'm worried that he forgot me." I try to pass it off as a joke, but I'm sure my furrowed brow gives me away.

"I've seen how that man looks at you. He won't forget." She gives my hand a pat. "I'm going to run and powder my nose. Will you be alright while I'm gone?"

"Yes, of course," I say distractedly, contemplating her words. Does Madden look at me a certain way?

After thirty more minutes, I'm the only one still sitting at our table. I realize Marie must have fallen into a conversation somewhere between here and the restroom and probably isn't coming back. I'm tired of sitting around by myself, so I get up and tour the perimeter of the room, looking at the modern artwork on the walls. Noticing a bar across the room from me, I head in that direction, hoping a glass of wine will take the edge off of my irritation. I place my order and just as the bartender hands me my glass, a young man appears at my side.

"Well, if it isn't Odette Windell, the belle of the ball. Congratulations on your marriage to Madden." He gives a little bow and flashes a charming smile, showing the dimple in his chin.

"Oh, thank you." There's something incredibly familiar about his tall stature, curly brown hair, and blue eyes. "And you are?"

He chuckles. "Christopher Highman. We met briefly at Bennington and Associates back in December."

Ah. Madden's old coworker. After seeing Larry in person now, it's hard to believe he has such a handsome son. Although not nearly as handsome as Madden. I extend my hand. "Oh, of course! Nice to see you again."

He gives my hand a gentle squeeze. "Surely you're not all alone this evening? Where is that husband of yours?" He quickly glances around the room in search of Madden.

"I'm afraid so. For the moment, anyway. Madden has a lot of people to speak with this evening." I look down at my wineglass.

"Well, just my luck!" Christopher takes my glass and sets it on the nearest table, then grabs my hand and leads me toward the dance floor.

"Oh, no, I couldn't. I promised Madden a dance first."

"He waited too long." He winks. "Plus, wouldn't it make Madden look fantastic if you had the kindness to dance with the son of the man he's running against?"

I pause. It *would* reflect well on Madden to behave kindly toward his opposition. And isn't that my job in this marriage: to make Madden look good? I sigh and nod. "I suppose you have a point."

And that's all the encouragement he needs to whisk me onto the dance floor. Much to my chagrin, the next dance is a slow song. Having Christopher's hands on my waist definitely feels a little strange. He holds me much too close for my comfort.

"So, is Madden as busy as my father with this campaign? I swear he eats, sleeps, and breathes this stuff." Christopher says with a roll of his eyes.

"He's very busy with the campaign, yes," I respond with a tight smile. "He takes it seriously, as he should."

Christopher raises an eyebrow. "Yes, I suppose that's true. I should probably cut my father some slack. How did you and Madden end up together, anyway?"

I start a bit at the abruptness of the question but manage to make it look like I tripped over my feet. "We both attended Heartland Academy, but didn't see each other again until last year."

"When you bumped into each other in D.C.?" He raises a skeptical eyebrow.

"You seem very familiar with my marriage, Mr. Highman." What is he getting at?

"Please, call me Christopher. And I don't mean to make you uncomfortable. I read about the two of you in that Washington Journal op-ed. It's a very *romantic* story."

I flash a confident smile. "Yes, we bumped into each other at a coffee shop and enjoyed catching up. Madden is so handsome and charming that it didn't take long to fall in love with him."

"No, not long at all." Christopher smirks.

An uncomfortable thought occurs to me, twisting my stomach into knots. Christopher's line of questioning seems oddly specific. Did Larry Highman send him on a mission to dance with me and collect information about Madden? Or does he know something about us already?

He pulls me a little closer and whispers, "If I were him, I would've proposed then and there and not waited another year."

I pull back in disbelief at his obvious flirtation and throw my gaze around the room, searching for some way out of this dance. My eyes meet the bright, angry blue eyes of my husband from across the dance floor. I very much dislike being on the receiving end of that look. I've never seen him angry before.

Christopher follows my gaze and guffaws, eyes narrowing on Madden. "Oh, dear. Someone does not enjoy seeing his lovely wife dancing with another man, does he? I guess he'll pay more attention to you next time."

Thankfully, before I can slap Christopher across his smug face, the dance ends and my fuming husband comes marching toward us.

"May I cut in?" Madden growls through bared teeth. I believe he's attempting to smile.

"Of course! So happy you've finally come to dance with your wife. She was awfully lonely when I found her."

Madden's jaw clenches.

Christopher must value his life because he quickly takes off and leaves us alone. But now that angry, wolfish smile is directed at me. "What are you doing?"

I grimace at his sharp tone. "Madden, calm down. He just asked me to dance. He said it would show solidarity between our families in spite of the election."

"And you believed him? He was probably trying to get information out of you to use against me." He says through gritted teeth.

"*I* thought it would reflect well on you. And heaven forbid that a nice man might ask me to dance without ill intent," I reply, trying unsuccessfully to hide my anger.

"First of all, Christopher isn't nice. Secondly, I told you I would dance with you. You could've been a little more patient," he hisses, trying not to draw attention to our argument.

My head rears back in shock. He did *not* just say that. "Madden, I've been waiting for *hours*. Forgive me if I don't believe your promises so easily. They've been forgotten before."

His jaw drops. "We're leaving *now*. I will not argue with my wife at a public event."

Madden hardly waits for the dance to end before he drags me toward the exit. We ride in silence to our apartment. I don't dare speak, hoping the drive home will allow him time to calm down and think rationally.

⤛

It's almost ten once we walk through the front door. I just want to go to sleep and put this awful night behind us, but I hear Madden loudly drop his wallet and keys onto the dining table and know that I'm in for a brawl.

"So, is this how it's going to be?" He throws his hands up.

I sigh. "What on earth do you mean?"

"Whenever I don't pay enough attention to you, you go find another man to entertain you?" His jaw twitches in anger.

I cross my arms across my chest defensively. "That is preposterous, and you know it. I already told you why I accepted his invitation to dance. Where is all of this coming from?"

His eyes pierce mine. I see anger in his gaze but also sadness, like I've wounded him. He whispers, "I hate feeling jealous and paranoid."

"Madden, I'm sorry that you're hurt. Surely you know I would never betray you, and if you don't know me well enough by now to trust my character then I don't know how we'll ever keep up this facade." I'm trying to keep emotions out of my voice, but my eyes betray me as one hot tear runs down my cheek.

Madden slowly turns and walks down the hallway to his room, closing the door softly behind him.

This evening has utterly exhausted me, physically and emotionally. I head to my room and draw a hot bath. I don't know how I'm going to get a wink of sleep tonight, knowing that Madden is stewing just down the hallway. But there's nothing more I can do.

Chapter 21

Madden

♥

It seems like the only thing I do in bed anymore is lie awake staring at the ceiling, thinking of all the dumb things I've said and done. I am kicking myself for letting my anger get the better of me. Odette is honest and kind. I *know* that, and I know she's telling the truth about Christopher.

That little son of a biscuit. Part of me wanted to punch him when I saw his hands on my wife's waist and his head leaning in to whisper in her ear. A larger part of me just felt stupid that I wasn't the one holding her in the first place.

With a groan, I roll over and flick on the lamp on my nightstand.

I've spent most of my life controlling my emotions and keeping myself in check. Since Odette came into my life, though, my thoughts are a constant kaleidoscope. I can't seem to gain control over them.

Needing something to distract myself, I reach for the stress management book I purchased last week.

If Odette desired attention, it's my fault for not giving her the attention she needed. I am so confused about my feelings for her. Some days I just want to give into them, but I've kept my heart under lock and key for so long, I'm not sure I still know how.

After re-reading the same sentence in my book ten times, I finally give up and set it back on the nightstand. I might as well get up and get a glass of warm milk. That always used to work when I was a kid.

Using my phone as a flashlight, I pad out into the kitchen and turn on the overhead light. I grab the milk, a loaf of bread, and some jam out of the fridge. While the bread is crisping in the toaster, I fill a glass with milk. Just as I'm about to take a sip, I hear a sound behind me. Before I can look over my shoulder, I hear Odette shriek.

"Madden! Why on earth aren't you dressed?" Her voice is high-pitched, almost a scream.

I look down, realizing that I'm just wearing my black boxer briefs. I'm equally amused and annoyed by her reaction. "Am I not allowed to walk around in underwear in my own home?"

Her gaze is defiant. "According to the contract, it's my house, too. For another year and a half, at least."

I'm about to respond with another saucy comeback when I catch myself. Why am I goading her when I should be apologizing? I internally kick myself again. This woman makes me crazy. "Actually, I'm glad you're up. I owe you an apology." I clear my throat. "My anger earlier was completely unwarranted. I was way out of line."

"And you think one quick apology can make everything better? You completely overreacted to me simply *dancing* with another man."

"You're right," I reply, causing her expression to turn from anger to surprise. "Whether I want to admit it or not, I... I've developed feelings for you." With a groan, I anxiously scrub my hands down my face. "I didn't like seeing Christopher's hands on you."

Her eyes soften as she looks at me, all anger now dissipated. "I have feelings for you too, Madden. But you don't see me biting the head off of every woman who shakes your hand."

A smile tugs at the corner of my mouth. "Very true. You have shown me over and over again that I can trust you. I will try my hardest not to react so strongly in the future."

"Okay." She hesitates, her eyes shifting down to my exposed chest. "So, are you going to put some clothes on?"

I shrug and chuckle. "They're just boxers."

"*Fine.* Two can play that game." Without hesitation, she unties her robe and lets it drop to the floor, leaving her in nothing but tiny silk shorts and a matching camisole.

My jaw drops. I was not expecting that. She walks right past me with complete confidence and pours herself a glass of milk.

"Odette…" I stutter as I take in her long, gorgeous legs and what seems like miles of smooth, pale flesh. I've never seen a woman so lovely. Odette is like a pearl amidst a pile of jagged rock, smooth, flawless, innocent.

I blink to regain my composure and bring my gaze back up to Odette's face. Her eyes twinkle with mischief, and my heart lurches in my chest. Odette hardly ever shows this feisty side of herself. I won't lie: it is extremely appealing. My resolve to fight the attraction between us is getting weaker by the second. Internally, I urge myself to go back to my room, but my body has other ideas. I take a step toward her.

This clearly surprises Odette, and she slowly backs away from me, a blush rushing to her cheeks as her confident facade fades back to shyness.

"Madden…" Her voice sounds low and raspy.

I take another step toward her. The gap between us grows smaller. With every step, her smooth skin looks more tempting, and her green eyes more alluring.

Odette gulps as I take a final step toward her, bringing us face to face. I look down at her captivating lips. "I've tried to keep my distance. I have. But I'm not sure that I can anymore." I run the back of my hand down the soft skin on her arm. I lean my head down so low the tips of our noses are almost touching. "It's killing me, Odette."

Her hands come up to rest hesitantly on my bare chest. Her voice is barely above a whisper. "What about the contract?"

Her touch is soft, but her eyes are filled with heat. The smell of her shampoo mixed with her own heady scent is so enticing. "I don't want to think about the contract. I just want to think about this."

I close the final distance, slowly running the tip of my nose down the side of her neck, and then I kiss my way toward her collarbone. She shivers, but her skin doesn't feel cold. She feels like fire.

I don't want to stop. Kissing Odette's skin is intoxicating. Through the haze in my mind, though, I sense that we're teetering on the edge of something big. If we fall into the unknown, I don't know what will happen to us. Should we put a stop to this?

Part of me hopes that Odette will make the decision for me by pushing me away. Instead, she slides her hands from my chest to my shoulders and links them around my neck. She wets her lips and leans forward.

I can't hold back any longer. I meet her the rest of the way and gently brush my lips against hers. Our lips move together like they were made for each other. I could kiss this woman for days and never grow tired of it. My hands go to her hips, eagerly pulling her body closer to mine.

Before either of us realizes it, we are kissing our way back to the master bedroom.

Odette

I wake up the next morning to sunlight peeking through the curtains and birds chirping outside the window. This seems like an unusually delightful morning. Is it just me or does the sunlight seem warmer and the birdsong happier? My body feels so relaxed. I clearly slept well last night. I shrug and let out a yawn.

That's when I notice the large, muscled arm wrapped around my waist.

The night before comes flooding back to me: meeting Madden in the kitchen, how he looked so muscular in his boxer briefs, the way my skin tingled when he kissed my neck... A hot blush starts at my toes and spreads all the way up to my hairline. Despite my embarrassment, I cautiously lean into him and close my eyes. There's something very comforting about having his arms wrapped around me.

Will things continue like this every night? I don't know where Madden's thoughts are. Did last night mean anything to him?

I blow out a deep breath. Who knew developing feelings for one's husband could be so complicated?

Madden's arm tightens around my waist, and his lips find my bare shoulder. "Good morning, Red. No need to blush. We *are* married, after all."

I let out a happy little sigh as Madden continues kissing up my shoulder, then my neck. "Did you sleep okay?" I giggle.

"I've never slept better," he replies huskily.

Rolling over so we're face to face, I take a minute to study his features. I'm not used to seeing him first thing in the morning before he showers and shaves, but I love how he looks right now with his hooded, sleepy eyes, stubbled chin, and mussed hair. I have a feeling that he doesn't allow many people to see him looking so unkempt, and that makes this moment feel extra special.

"What's going on in there?" He gently taps my temple. "You look deep in thought."

I run a hand through his hair, loving the way his thick waves feel on my fingertips. "I was just thinking how handsome you are first thing in the morning."

He smirks. "Maybe you should see me first thing *every* morning, then."

"Does that mean you're willing to give this a chance? For real?" I bite my bottom lip nervously.

Madden pulls me closer. "I think so. Let's see where this goes, okay?"

"Okay." I bring my lips to his.

Madden cancels all his appointments for the day.

Chapter 22

Madden

♥

I 've slept next to my wife for the last two weeks, and going to bed has quickly become my favorite part of each day. Our communication has grown, and she seems happy.

I want to enjoy this as blissfully as she clearly is, but something deep down keeps inching its way to the surface, nagging me.

Fear of failure, maybe.

The closer I feel to Odette, the more I slack off in my campaign. I canceled an appearance at the county library just to spend a day in bed with her, and instead of spending hours networking with constituents after events, I left each one as early as possible, anxious to come home to her.

What if being in a real relationship with Odette makes me a terrible congressman?

I scrub my hands down my face and sigh. It's only been two weeks. Hopefully, this pit in my stomach will fade with time. Because Odette makes me happier than I've felt in a really long time.

With my hectic campaign schedule–and our recent fascination with each other–we've hardly spent any time with our families. We decided to change that today. Odette spent the day with her parents while I wrote some speeches, and I'm on my way now to pick them up for dinner and a game night at my parents' house.

After picking up Odette and her parents, I drive across town to my parent's house. I park in the driveway and, after helping Mr. Hastings out of the vehicle, I watch him walk steadily to the front door, using just his cane. I smile at my wife, who's looking at her dad with pure joy.

Mrs. Hastings links her arm through Odette's as we walk up the path to the front door. From behind me, I faintly hear Mrs. Hasting whisper to Odette, "Your father and I adore seeing you so in love, sweetheart. Nothing could make us happier."

I nearly trip over the front steps. Love? I know we have feelings for each other, but surely she's not in love?

Mom meets us at the door and shuffles us into the dining room, looking pinched and irritated.

"Okay, everyone's here now. Let's eat." She takes a seat at the head of the table.

I glance at my brothers around the dining table. "Where's Dad?"

Mom's eyes don't leave the chicken on her plate as she delicately slices into it. "He's at the hospital. He agreed to do a last-minute surgery."

Odette looks over at me with a grimace and shrugs.

Thankfully, Brooks breaks the awkward silence. "Speaking of surgeries, have you heard the story about when Madden stuck a pencil up his nose and the eraser broke off and got stuck?"

Odette and her parents laugh, and I can't decide whether to be grateful or to throttle him for telling that story. But I let him continue entertaining the Hastings at my expense. It's just nice to see everyone enjoying themselves.

I wasn't sure how my wife would behave around me in front of our families, but she seems totally at ease and affectionate. I keep my arm around her for most of the evening, ignoring the quizzical looks my family keeps shooting at us. I'm not sure I could keep my hands off of her, even if I wanted to.

We all move to the living room when dinner wraps up. Odette rests her hand on my leg as we sit side by side on the sofa. Brooks enters the room with a sly grin on his face, carrying a tattered Monopoly board game. David jumps up from his seat to intercept him.

"Absolutely not."

"Oh, come on! It's been forever!" Brooks whines.

"You know why it has been forever, Brooks," I call out from the sofa.

"That won't happen again! It's just a game."

David glances warily around the room. "We can't do this in front of Odette and her parents."

Brooks glares at David. "Well, we *could* if you'd just behave and *not* hulk out on one of Mom's vases again."

Mom steps between the two like a referee and reaches for the game. "Hand it over. Especially since Sophie isn't here to keep the peace between you three ogres."

Brooks holds the game higher so she can't reach it. "Come on, Mom! We will be on our best behavior."

Mom quirks an eyebrow at David. "You and I both know that *someone* takes the game a little too seriously since attaining his CPA license."

David's jaw drops dramatically. "That was not my fault! The IRS would've caught the underhanded deals those two were making in a heartbeat."

I can tell Odette is trying not to laugh, but her parents look a little concerned as my brothers practically bare their teeth at each other. The Hastings probably had a much calmer home than this, raising one child.

Our argument fades after a few more minutes and finally, Brooks agrees to put away the Monopoly game. We manage to agree on The Game of Life. Even Mr. Hastings joins in.

By the end of the game, mine and Odette's Life vehicles are full of children, and our mothers cannot stop giggling about it.

"Odette tells me that Sophie is having a baby girl! How delightful." Mrs. Hastings says to my Mom.

Mom beams with excitement. "Oh, I cannot wait! I have bags upon bags of pink, ruffled outfits already."

"I'm sure I'll be the same way when Madden and Odette have children. We cannot wait to be grandparents!"

The blood drains from my face. My mom glances in my direction then chuckles awkwardly, but quickly smooths her features and changes the subject.

She knows that the Hastings have no idea about our contract.

But Mrs. Hastings' comment leaves me tense. My relationship with my wife has definitely come a long way, and yet we've never discussed children. Just the thought overwhelms me. I already feel like my life is a balancing act between my campaign and being a husband. But children? Sweat begins to form on my brow.

Odette must notice my panic because she gently places her hand on my knee. But the nagging fear of failure is back in full force throughout the rest of the evening.

After a few more games of Life, we drop off Odette's parents and drive back to our apartment in silence.

Finally mustering up the bravery to speak, I lean against the open doorway in Odette's room. "Odette." I pause and release a deep breath. "Do you want children? If we make this marriage work, I mean."

"Is this about my mom's comment?" She sighs and comes up beside me, running her hands down my arms. "Honestly, I always pictured myself having children, but it's not something I expect immediately."

Of course she wants children. My stomach drops. Bringing my chin to my chest, I rub the back of my neck. "When we talked about seeing where this goes, I hadn't even considered children."

"You don't want kids? Ever?"

"This is a lot of pressure, Odette." I massage my temples with my fingertips. "I'm running for Congress. I don't know how to be the kind of politician that I want to be *and* the kind of husband you need at the same time. I'm not sure that's even possible. And then adding a child to all of that?"

"That's ridiculous. Lots of people juggle successful careers *and* families. It's not rocket science."

An image of my parents bickering in the kitchen at Thanksgiving flashes through my mind. "It is to me."

"You're not even willing to *try*?" Her pained expression guts me.

I swallow. "Maybe we were getting a little ahead of ourselves." I don't want to hurt her, but I'd rather take the time to really think about this now rather than down the road. What if we're not actually as compatible as we thought? "This is all moving too fast. I think I just need some space."

I walk past her into the room and grab my pillow from her bed.

She tugs at my sleeve, a tear running down her cheek. "Madden, you're looking too far ahead. We don't have to know these things yet. Please, talk to me."

Gently, I pull my arm away. "We will. I just need some time to think, okay?"

I walk slowly toward the guest room. The look of hurt on her face as I turn away constricts my chest, and I have to remind myself to breathe.

Chapter 23

Madden

♥

Early the next morning, I wake up to my iPhone ringing loudly next to my bed. I blink a few times, feeling slightly disoriented that I'm in the guest room alone instead of by Odette's side.

Then I remember last night.

Groaning, I grab my phone off the nightstand and bring it to my ear. Before I can even mumble a greeting, David yells through the receiver, "Have you seen Highman's new commercial?"

I wince. "What? No. I just woke up." I glance at the clock on my nightstand and see that it's barely past seven.

David sighs in annoyance. "Look it up on YouTube right now."

"Okay, okay. Grabbing my computer now." I rub my eyes as I roll out of bed and walk to my desk. Opening my MacBook, I type YouTube into the search box and bring up the link to Highman's commercial.

The four-minute clip shows a montage of photos and videos, all from my dating rampage last year. I furrow my brow. Had someone been following me?

The narrator's voice speculates that I was looking for a wife to make myself look like a better candidate, then sticks the landing by flashing over screenshots of the documents Odette and I signed at Bennington and Associates. The commercial ends and the screen goes gray, pulling up a list of recommended videos.

I sit in stunned silence. "This is bad."

"Bad is an understatement unless you're trying to become the next Bachelor," David growls. "How did they get copies of those documents?"

"I don't know." I run my hand through my hair. "I need to get a hold of Richard Bennington."

"We need to figure out how to spin this."

"How to *spin* this? David, they have the legal documents. They know what I did."

"Yes, but you and Odette *are* married. We can prove that your wedding was real. And you've been seen in public together for months now. We can find a way to salvage this."

I hear someone banging at my apartment's front door and take a deep breath. "I need to go. I'll call you back later."

We hang up and I throw some clothes on. By the time I reach the front door, Odette has beaten me there, already awake and dressed for the day. I should've anticipated that she'd be awake. She's an early riser.

Odette looks at me uncomfortably as Paul storms through the door. "You've seen it?" He says, unsuccessfully disguising his anger.

I rub my temples. "David just called. What are we going to do?"

Odette looks between Paul and I in confusion. "Wait, what's going on?"

Turning on the TV, I open up the YouTube app and play the commercial for her. Her mouth gapes open in shock. "How did they get our private documents?" And then her shock turns into annoyance. "And how come every woman you went out with was blonde?"

I glare at her. "That is *clearly* beside the point. This is a disaster." I throw my hands up and pace back and forth across the living room.

"Okay, let's take a deep breath. Who might've had access to your marriage contract?" Paul asks.

I think for a moment, but the answer hits me within seconds. "Christopher Highman. It had to be him. He works for Bennington *and* I'm running against his father."

"You need to get your lawyer on this ASAP," Paul states.

Suddenly, my phone buzzes in my back pocket. I pull it out and check the caller ID. "Speak of the devil." I raise the phone to my ear. "Good morning, Richard. If you're calling to tell me that our marriage contract was somehow leaked, you're a little late."

"I can't tell you how sorry I am, Madden." Richard's voice is deeply contrite. "You know how seriously we take our clients' privacy. For this to happen under my watch is absolutely unpardonable."

"I understand, but that doesn't help us now. Can you at least tell me how this happened?"

He hesitates. "I'm sure you can guess. I searched Christopher's office and found a printed copy of your marriage contract in the top drawer of his desk. He must have found a way to hack into my computer and download the files. Obviously, I will address this security threat and take the necessary steps to reprimand Christopher."

"By that, I hope you mean that you're firing him. And filing a civil suit."

"We'll handle it."

I run my fingers through my hair. "I can't believe he'd be willing to ruin his career just to mess up my campaign. I always knew he didn't like me, but this seems extreme."

"Well, Larry Highman has been planning to run for Congress for years. He made no secret of that. When you mentioned running, he must have hired a private investigator to follow you, which explains the photos."

I groan. "Thanks for letting me know."

Richard sighs. "I'm so sorry, Madden. I know what this campaign means to you."

I can't speak past the lump in my throat. I hang up and look at Paul and Odette's grim faces.

Odette shakes her head. "I guess you were right to question his character."

"Well, I *had* worked with him for years."

"I wonder what will happen now. For all the damage this may inflict on you, it will reflect very poorly on Larry's campaign." Paul rubs his chin.

"Yeah, Kansans has two impeccable choices this year, huh? A playboy liar and a corrupt scumbag."

Odette bites her lip as she thinks. "Obviously, this is very upsetting, but scandals *do* come out during political campaigns all the time, even in small-scale elections. Smear campaigns have become so commonplace that sometimes people don't even believe what they hear about political candidates."

"But the documents are already out there. The media can verify them."

Odette puts a hand on my arm. "I'm just saying that maybe we should wait and see how the public reacts before we do anything crazy. For now, we could make a commercial of your own. We can show the public your true character and try to draw attention away from the marriage contract."

She crosses the room to grab a pen and notebook. "Madden's commercial could show how he stands up for families and education. We have *tons* of photos and videos of us reading to the kids on Kansas Day and speaking at the immigration charity, not to mention our photoshoot with the Washington Journal." She starts jotting down her ideas in the notebook and then blushes, probably remembering our kiss. "That could help squash the marriage contract rumors."

"But they aren't rumors." I point out, angry at myself for ever coming up with this plan. "I *did* try to deceive the public."

"We don't have time for a moral crisis right now. Listen to your wife." Paul turns to Odette, his expression revealing how impressed he is. "When you're done with Madden, young lady, please come work for me."

When you're done with Madden. Paul's statement rings in my ears. My heart sinks. Those words alone hit me harder than news of the commercial did. Odette has been invaluable to my campaign, of course, but she's been even more impressive in our relationship. No matter how many times I push her away and act like a total idiot, she holds up her end of our agreement.

A memory flashes through my mind. Whenever my parents used to argue, my mom completely shut my Dad out, usually hiding in her room. But Odette hasn't run away. She's here instead, problem-solving with Paul and I in spite of how much I hurt her last night.

"Are there any photos of the two of you in high school? I'd love to paint a picture of you both being friends before you got married. We can show the public that you two have known each other for years."

"We were on the debate team together, so there should be some photos." My voice sounds tired in my own ears. "I'll head to my parent's house and look. My mom keeps everything."

≈

Odette

The apartment is quiet now as I lay on my bed staring up at the ceiling. Alone. Madden and Paul left soon after Richard Bennington's call, hell-bent on finding high school photos at his parents' house.

Loneliness hasn't been an unfamiliar feeling in my life, growing up without siblings and then being single for so long. But it's amazing how quickly I grew accustomed to not being lonely anymore. These last few weeks, I felt cherished.

And then Madden went to sleep in the guest room last night. Sleeping alone in the master bedroom without him felt cold and empty.

That feeling only intensified when I woke up to this news. Can our marriage withstand this kind of public scrutiny? We're already struggling as it is.

I should probably brainstorm other ways to help Madden's campaign survive, but I can't focus. If the public turns against us, we've lost the election before it even begins. What will be the point of our marriage then? If all of this is bound to end soon, I need a backup plan.

I need a job.

I sit up on my king bed and pull my laptop open. It's about time I do some research on freelance assisting. I've been stuck in this mindset, feeling down on myself because I'm nearly thirty and have no idea where my life is headed. Meeting the needs of my parents and Madden helped give me purpose, but it was just a smokescreen. I lost myself somewhere in this process.

I don't know how long I sit there scouring job listings, glasses perched on my nose, a pencil stuck in my messy bun, and notebooks surrounding me. Suddenly, I hear the front door open and close. Madden's footsteps grow louder until there's a gentle knock on my door.

"Come in," I say hesitantly, not looking forward to being alone with Madden after last night.

He opens the door and his eyes fly open as he takes in the notebooks on the bed. "What's all this?"

"I was doing research on freelance political assisting."

"Oh." His mouth twists in irritation. "I thought maybe you'd take Paul up on his job offer."

I shrug, feeling a bit defensive. "If our marriage ends soon, I need to figure out what the next step is for me."

"We're in the middle of a crisis, and this was the first thing you decided to do?"

"What do you expect me to do?" I retort with a little more sass than I intended.

"I *am* sorry about last night. The thought of having children was... unexpected." He awkwardly shuffles from one foot to the other. "But just because I need space doesn't mean I'm ready to give up on us."

I watch him skeptically. He's so hot and cold sometimes that I don't know if I should trust what he says.

"The tension between us is unbearable. And I despise sleeping alone." Madden runs his hands through his hair nervously. "I can barely sleep without you by my side now."

Is he serious? He just wants a bed buddy? "You can't keep going back and forth like this. I'm sorry that you *despise* sleeping alone, but you're the one who chose that."

"It's not just about our sleeping arrangement. Listen, when I was with Jen... I felt... I don't know." He sighs in frustration. "It's really difficult for me to open up and be vulnerable now."

"I hate that she broke your heart," I say, my voice is softer now. "But if you're not willing to be vulnerable, you'll never even have the *chance* for a successful relationship."

Madden nods. "I know you're right. It's just a slow process. I wish I'd at least had a good example of a loving marriage growing up like you did. My parents despise each other."

I grimace. "I have noticed some tension there. "

He begins to speak but then stops himself, struggling for words. Finally, he says, "When Jen ended things, she said I'm just like my dad, that I always put my work first and never prioritize her... I've never told anyone she said that, but it... it ripped me up inside." He looks up at me with exhausted eyes. "I don't want to hurt you."

"That's awful, Madden. I'm so sorry she said that to you." I think for a few seconds before speaking. "But what if by pushing me away, you're proving her right? Just because your mom resents your dad doesn't mean that has to be your future as well."

"I've been wondering about that myself, lately." He breathes a shuddering sigh. "But I'm trying to change. Will you be patient with me?"

My eyebrows draw together as I think. "Honestly, it's hard for me to be patient. You give up on us so easily." I close my eyes to keep my tears from falling. "Madden, I want it all. I want a marriage filled with love, a house with children running around, and a husband who's willing to give 110% when necessary–someone I can trust my heart with." My voice cracks. "And *you* are the only man I've ever been able to picture that life with. I know that wasn't the original purpose of our marriage, but... I think we could be happy."

Madden walks over and sits on the edge of the bed. "I *want* to try to be that man for you, Odette. I may have ruined this, but I don't want to lose you."

"I'm glad you're willing to try," I say quietly. "But maybe *I* need some space now."

Disappointment flits across his face. "If that's what you want–"

Madden stops talking abruptly when I hear my phone ring. I see it's my mom and my shoulders tense. I answer quickly. "Hello?"

"Sweetheart." Her voice sounds strained. "We were watching the morning news, and they said something about leaked documents. About you and Madden."

My stomach drops. I'm not ready to have this conversation with my parents. I look over at Madden, his expression one of grim concern. He's sitting close enough to hear our conversation. "Mom, Madden's campaign team is working hard to–"

"They're saying that your marriage is a business arrangement. Is that true?"

"Mom..."

"I went into our assisted living office and asked them what arrangements you made for payments. They said it wasn't under your name *or* our names. And didn't you tell us Medicare was footing the bill?"

I close my eyes and breathe slowly. "I didn't want you to be embarrassed, but we couldn't afford assisted living, and... Madden offered me a deal."

"So you two aren't really married? You never were?"

I swallow. Tears build up in my eyes. "We *are* married... It just wasn't for love." Out of the corner of my eye, I see Madden hang his head in shame. "We were out of options. I just wanted you and Dad to be taken care of."

She bursts into tears. "Your Dad and I would've figured something out! Odette, how could you lie to us?"

Now the tears stream down my face. "I'm so sorry."

"It's not supposed to be this way. *We* are your parents. We're supposed to take care of *you*."

"Mom, can we please talk about this in person? I want to explain."

"Okay." She hangs up.

I stare at my phone, tears falling into my lap. Madden doesn't say anything. What is there to say? Instead, he pulls me into a hug and lets me cry on his shoulder.

Chapter 24

Madden

♥

After hustling for two days, we managed to collect everything we needed to shoot our own commercial. I even found two photos of me and Odette in my yearbook from our Heartland debate team days. Miraculously, we're standing next to each other in one of them. When I study the photo, I see that Odette was just as gorgeous back then–even with her frizzy hair–but I was too immature to see it.

The pictures are just what we need to prove that we knew each other before getting engaged in December.

Odette and I arrive at the small studio where I hired a highly recommended videographer to put the commercial together. Paul and David are already there waiting for us. The room is filled with large tables, computer screens, and many dials and cranks, which I have no clue how to work. There's a viewing area with a few chairs and a large TV screen. We gather around to watch the completed commercial for the first time.

The commercial begins with a wedding photo of me and Odette superimposed over an American flag.

"Madden Windell," the narrator's smooth voice begins. "Your Kansas congressman for immigration–"

The word *Immigration* pops up in the next shot, then fades into a clip of my speech at the immigration charity banquet.

"–military support–" The image fades to the words *Military Support*, then displays a photo of me with Sophie and her husband

Sam in his military uniform.

"–and education." Then the word *Education* appears with a photo of me and Odette dressed up on Kansas Day, surrounded by students holding sunflower drawings in the school gymnasium. When that photo fades, a video of me reading to the kindergarten class comes on against a backtrack of patriotic music. Lastly, the video flips through a slideshow of photos, showing me at various charity events and political campaigns.

"Madden Windell," the narrator says again. "Caring, hardworking, and for the people. Vote Windell for Kansas." The screen fades to black.

"This turned out great! Thank you so much." I shake the videographer's hand, then turn to my wife. "And thank you, Odette, for your ideas. We couldn't have put this together without you."

"Thanks. Maybe I'll run against you in the next election," she teases. I laugh, drawing David's and Paul's attention. "What do you two think of Odette running in the next election? *I'd* vote for her."

David smirks at me. "Me too. She'd probably be a better candidate than you." His smug smile quickly disappears as I cross the room and put him in a headlock.

"Okay, children." Paul rolls his eyes as he pulls me off of David. "Hopefully, this will diffuse the situation. Let's pray that Highman doesn't have any other tricks up his sleeve."

"Surely he can just focus on his own campaign now," I grumble.

Paul shrugs. "You don't have many skeletons in your closet, so to speak. I'm not sure what else he could use against you."

"And if he does, we have our secret weapon." David smiles, motioning toward Odette.

"Speaking of which, I think you two need to amp up the public appearances. At this point, you cannot be seen together too much.

Also, we're going to need more PDA," Paul says, looking between Odette and I.

Odette turns bright red at the mention of PDA, especially since things are still a little tense between us. Reaching for her hand, I give it a squeeze. "It'll be alright. We'll make it work."

⤳

Odette

After leaving the videographer's studio, Madden and I drive to my parents' place. I've tried to convince myself that the reason we didn't see them sooner was because of the commercial, but I know that's not entirely true. Honestly, I just didn't want to face them.

We're quiet during the drive, both deep in thought. I sigh as I look out the window at the passing city lights. I appreciate Madden's willingness to come with me and explain things to my parents. I can tell that he's trying to mend our relationship, but I don't know if it's possible.

The unfortunate truth is that I'm already in love with him, but he has been so back and forth from the start. I need to protect myself. Being physically and emotionally close to him would be too challenging for me when he clearly doesn't know what he wants out of our marriage. Of course, his original goal was just to make it to Congress and perhaps have an amicable relationship, but now he seems confused. If we're going to do this, though, I need him to be all in. It hurts too much to be stuck somewhere in the middle.

We pull up to my parents' home and walk to the door, knocking hesitantly. It takes a minute—which feels more like an hour—but my dad finally answers. His usually pleasant demeanor is gone, replaced with a sour expression. He steps out of the way so we can enter. "Come in."

Mom is seated on the sofa, her skin sallow and her button-up shirt and khakis wrinkled. It looks like she rolled right out of bed. She looks up at me with weary eyes but says nothing. Dad takes a seat next to her, and I sit in the armchair across from them.

Madden stays standing and takes a deep breath. "Mr. and Mrs. Hastings, I take full responsibility for all of this. Our marriage was supposed to be a simple business transaction. My campaign research suggested that Kansans would be more likely to vote for me if I had a wife." He sinks into the armchair next to mine. "I knew that your family was in a tight spot and I... I took advantage of that. Odette wanted to take care of you both, and I needed a wife. So I offered to help out financially if she'd marry me and attend political events on my arm. We always intended to end it once we had helped each other. We didn't mean to hurt anyone."

My parents are silent for a long while after Madden's speech. Finally, my mom shakes her head. "But marriage isn't a business transaction. It's supposed to be a commitment to love each other for your whole lives." She turns to me suddenly, her eyes brimming with unshed tears. "Odette, I know we put too much on you. But you didn't even talk to us about this. Even worse, you *lied*."

I wince and hang my head, unable to look at my mom. Madden clears his throat beside me. "I'm afraid that part is my fault, too. We signed a nondisclosure agreement to protect my public reputation."

Dad pins Madden with a serious look. "Did it ever cross your mind that if it has to be kept a secret, it probably isn't a good idea?"

"What happens after he's elected? Will you end your marriage?" Mom asks.

Nervously, I play with a strand of hair that escaped from my messy bun. "Yes."

Mom's jaw drops in horror. "But why? It's obvious that you two truly care about each other."

Madden gently places his hand on my knee. "I *have* grown to care for Odette, deeply. But I can't expect her to sacrifice her goals and ambitions for mine." He glances at me out of the corner of his eye. "We're taking our time to figure things out."

Dad scoffs. "Shouldn't you have done that *before* getting married??"

"You're right. I should've pursued Odette the proper way. And I should have never married someone just to further my career." Madden sighs. "It was wrong, and I wish I could go back and do things over. I'm genuinely sorry for the hurt I've caused."

I look over at Madden, unwilling to let him take all the blame. "This isn't all on you, Madden. It takes two people to enter a marriage. We both made a mistake."

Unable to hold in my tears any longer, I break down into sobs. Mom gets up and she kneels down in front of my chair, pulling my hands into hers. "You're our daughter. We will always love you, no matter what. But this hurt us."

Dad hesitantly joins us, wrapping his arms around me and Mom. When our embrace ends, he meets Madden's eyes coolly. "I'm not ready to hug you just yet, young man."

Madden nods. "Understandable, sir."

Chapter 25

Madden

♥

Over the next week, we wait to see how the public reacts to Larry's commercial as well as ours. Paul urged us to stay off the internet in the interim, probably hoping to shield us from the worst of the blowback. It's been killing me not to check and see what the media is saying.

Now on day seven, Paul and David are supposed to come over so we can review the data they've collected. Much to my frustration, they're an hour late and haven't responded to any of my phone calls.

I massage the back of my neck after another failed attempt to call Paul.

"Still not answering?" Odette asks nervously. She's anxious for them to arrive. This all affects her too. I can tell by her tired eyes that she's as stressed about this as I am. I desperately want to comfort her, but I promised her space.

I drag my hands through my hair. "Nope. I've tried his phone and David's at least a dozen times each."

A knock on our apartment door makes us jump. "Finally," I mutter as I stomp over to open it.

Paul and David walk through the door, sopping wet from the rain outside.

"Why on earth are you so wet? Did you go dancing in the rain or something?"

They look at each other with a grimace. "Not exactly," David says.

"What is it?" I look from David to Paul. "Just tell me."

"On the drive over here, we saw a bunch of your campaign signs. They had been vandalized..." Paul wipes his face uneasily. "And the few that hadn't were removed completely."

"Vandalized *how*?" I ask, my heart sinking.

"Someone took bright pink spray paint and wrote–" David clears his throat awkwardly "–*man-whore...* on them."

"So, should we order more signs? Or does this mean everyone in Kansas hates me?"

"It really doesn't look good, Madden," Paul says gently. "I'm sorry."

"It *did* just come out last night that Christopher Highman has a civil suit filed against him for releasing confidential documents," David offers. "So, things don't look great for Larry, either."

Odette must have noticed Paul and David dripping all over the tile because she moves suddenly to the linen closet for a few towels. "Here, dry yourselves off. Thanks for taking care of the signs, guys."

"Yes, thank you for taking care of it. I'm sure it was miserable in the rain." I sigh. "So what do we do now?"

Paul quickly dries his hair off with the towel, then drapes it around his shoulders. "Like David said, the news about Christopher hit the media yesterday, so we're not sure yet how this will affect Larry's campaign. What we do know is that, according to this week's polls, you're way behind Larry since his commercial came out."

"And the comments on social media are... vicious," David says quietly. "Several people compared you to a pimp and Odette to a.... well, a prostitute."

Odette's face pales.

Rage surges in my chest, followed quickly by shame. This is my fault. "I'm so sorry, Odette. I really hoped the commercial we made would help."

Paul brings his hand to Odette's shoulder. "Try to stay off of social media for a while yet... I was worried about how people might react. It's so easy to say horrible things about someone when you're hiding behind a screen. Don't let it weigh you down."

I move toward Odette and grab her hand, threading our fingers together. She stiffens at first, but the gesture must be comforting because, after a few seconds, she leans against me. "I want to make a public apology. I think that's all I can do at this point. I need to own up to my mistakes and be honest, not just because it might endear me to voters, but because it's the right thing to do."

Odette looks up at me, her green eyes brimming with tears. "I'll stand up with you. We both did this. We both lied."

Abruptly, we hear banging on the front door. I groan, expecting to see a journalist when I open it. Much to my surprise, it's my mother. She's soaked with rain and crying.

I pull her inside and wrap my arms around her. It's alarming to see her so upset. My mother has probably cried in front of me three times in my entire life. Something must be horribly wrong.

"Shh, Mom. It's okay." I whisper, trying to calm her, but her body is convulsing with heavy sobs. If my arms weren't holding her up, I'm positive she would collapse onto the floor.

David brings his towel over and covers her shoulder with it, alarm evident in his usually calm expression. "What's wrong?"

I pull back so I can look at her, but hold on to her shoulders firmly so she won't fall. She tries to calm herself, attempting to steady her breath. Finally, with tears still streaming down her face, she rasps, "It's Sam."

My face falls, and dread settles in the pit of my stomach. "What about Sam? What happened?"

"Is Sophie okay?" David asks, eyes wide with panic.

She takes another deep breath and manages to choke out between sobs, "He was killed... by an IED."

"No..." I must have misheard her, or maybe there's been some mistake. "That can't be right."

"Your dad is in surgery and I can't get a hold of him." She sits on the couch and grabs a box of tissues. "Sophie is distraught. She needs us."

I look over at Paul. "I'm sorry. The campaign will just have to wait. I hope you understand."

Paul simply nods and offers his condolences, then leaves. I see the grim look on his face as he shuts the door behind him, though. We both know that taking time away right now could prove even more detrimental to my chances. But if I've realized anything in the last few weeks, it's that there are many things more important than a person's career.

I turn back to my mom and nod. "I'll book us plane tickets to North Carolina tonight."

Looking up, I notice Odette standing a few feet away, looking pained and uncomfortable, like she's not sure what to do. The moment our eyes meet, the tears I've been holding back sting my eyes. Something about looking into her eyes makes me feel comfortable releasing this pent-up emotion. By the time the first tear rolls down my cheek, she is at my side with her arms wrapped around my waist and her head laid gently on my chest. I don't hesitate to wrap my arms around her shoulders and we simply stand there holding each other and crying together.

"Please come to North Carolina with me," I whisper into her hair.

"Of course I will," She replies without hesitation.

David offers to take Mom to the hospital so they can wait for Dad to finish his surgery. With his arm around her shoulders, they say their goodbyes and head out to David's car. Odette has the presence of mind to hand them an umbrella so they don't become drenched all over again.

I pull out my phone and begin looking for tickets, hoping we can fly out in the next few hours, while Odette packs our suitcases. I've never had anyone pack a suitcase for me before, at least since I've been an adult. But right now, all I can think of is my sister losing her husband and their unborn baby losing her father. The thought makes me want to vomit.

⬿

Three hours later, we all board our flight. Dad's surgery ended just as David and Mom arrived at the hospital, and Odette and I went to Brooks' house to tell him the devastating news. Thankfully, we all managed to get on the same flight.

Once we're in the air, I slide the armrest up and pull Odette into my side. She lays her head on my shoulder.

Kissing the top of her head, I breathe, "I'm sorry everything is a mess right now, but it means the world to mean that you were willing to come." I lean back so I can look into her eyes.

Odette closes the distance between us and touches her soft lips to mine briefly. "I'm sorry, too. And despite needing some space, I *do* care about you... Maybe too much."

It's my turn to kiss her. I slide my hand to the back of her neck and pull her closer as her hand comes up to caress the line of my jaw. Just as I tilt my head to the side so I have a better angle to kiss her, I hear the old lady seated next to Odette clear her throat. We sit up straight and glance at her just long enough to see her scowling back at us.

We land in Fayetteville, North Carolina, at 11:00 PM and take an Uber to Sophie's house. A few of her friends greet us at the door when we arrive, puffy-eyed and somber. Mom rushes straight inside to find Soph. It breaks my heart that she was completely alone when an officer—whom she probably didn't even know—knocked on her door and informed her of Sam's death.

Sophie's friends murmur their goodbyes and drift out the door as we make our way inside, giving us space to be with Sophie alone, I assume. Inside, the house is simple and clean. I can tell that Sophie enjoyed decorating and taking care of the place—at least until yesterday. Tonight, though, it's dark and smells stale, a scent I might expect from an old, abandoned house. This must be the smell that takes over when there's so much heartbreak in one small space.

We enter the living room and my heart squeezes painfully at the sight.

Sophie is disheveled, her eyes red and her face streaked with tear stains. I expected to find her sobbing, but she is completely silent. She just looks numb and a little angry. The swell of her pregnant belly shows underneath her baggy t-shirt, a painful reminder that Sophie's baby will never get to meet her father. Mom has her arms around my sister and Dad sits on the sofa next to them, rubbing her back. We all silently surround her, just letting her know we're here.

After an hour, Mom finally convinced my sister to go to bed and try to sleep. The rest of us grab whatever pillows and blankets we can find and lay down wherever we can conjure a comfortable spot. Odette quietly lies down next to me on the couch and I hold her tight. She doesn't fight it.

I'm pretty sure I could fall asleep anywhere, as long as she's in my arms.

⋅⋅⋅

Two days into our stay in North Carolina, it already feels like two weeks. We've spent all of our time helping Sophie make funeral arrangements and wrap up loose ends with her landlord so she can come home with us afterward. She was adamantly against staying in North Carolina by herself.

With Sam's funeral tomorrow, we spend today helping her pack up what she needs to fly home with us. The military movers will pack up the house and move the rest later. For now, she will move in with my parents, which I think is a good plan. As excited as we are to have Sophie back in Wichita, I hate the circumstances behind it.

Since Odette wanted to do some more packing, Sophie volunteered to come with me to get lunch for everyone. I imagine that she was ready to get out of the house.

We have barely started driving when she turns to me with a serious look on her face. "How are things going with Odette?"

"Soph, we don't have to talk about this."

"I want to. I'll go crazy if we talk about the funeral or the move or anything else about Sam. I want to talk about something else for just a minute. So, how are things going with Odette?"

I look over at her from the driver's seat. "What do you want to know, exactly?"

She crosses her arms. "When I saw you two in December, she could barely look at you. But over the last few days, I keep seeing the two of you stealing glances at each other. And don't think I didn't notice you guys snuggled up on the couch these past few mornings."

I chuckle. "Stealing glances?"

"Yeah, you know, those coy, flirtatious looks." She smiles cheekily, though it doesn't quite reach her eyes.

"Long story short, I wasted the first six months of our marriage trying not to develop feelings for her." I smile and shake my head at how ridiculous that sounds. "Obviously, it didn't work very well. I assumed I was too much like Dad to make her happy."

"What? You're nothing like Dad," she scoffs.

I hold up one hand and count on my fingers. "One, I'm super handsome. Two, I'm an overachieving perfectionist. Three, I work too much. Four–"

"I'll stop you right there. Yes, you're a hard worker, but you have never put work over family like Dad." She pauses. "Do you know how many times Dad forgot my birthday? *You* remembered, though, and called me every single year–even when you were in law school." She smiles at me, though her expression is suddenly forlorn. "And when I married Sam, you started calling him every year on his birthday, too."

We pull into the Bojangles drive-thru and wait in a line of cars. I place my hand on her shoulder. "I am so sorry, Soph."

She wipes a tear from her cheek. "I know. I am, too." She takes a deep breath. "Promise me something, though?"

"Of course, anything."

"Don't let your insecurities keep you from having an amazing marriage with Odette, okay? There's nothing like being married to your best friend. Don't take it for granted."

"I won't. Promise." I say with confidence because I'm determined to show her she can trust me with her heart.

On the drive back to Sophie's place, I ponder her comment. *There's nothing like being married to your best friend.* I realize with a start that Odette really has become my best friend. She's the first person I think about when I wake up and the first person I want to share good news with. She has been a balm to my closed-off heart and a breath of fresh air in a lifetime of busyness.

Something in my heart has changed since she walked into my life, like the molecules of my body have shifted, causing my heart to double in size. I miss her when she's only been away for a few hours; I find myself daydreaming about her smile, and I *have* to touch her every time she's nearby. She makes me want to be a better man, a man who deserves her and cares about her more than anything else in the world.

Oh, dear. I think I've gone and fallen in love with my wife.

Chapter 26

Odette

♥

Today was Sam's funeral, an equally devastating and beautiful day. Sophie wore a simple black maternity dress with little pink flowers on it. A few of Sam's comrades shared stories about him—which made my heart feel heavy because I never got to meet him—and then the other military spouses gathered around Sophie to comfort her during the burial. When the trumpeter played "Taps", she finally cried, breaking down in excruciating sobs. I don't think she took her hand off her belly the entire day except for when they handed her Sam's flag.

At 9:00 PM, Madden and I take an Uber to our hotel. I rub my lower back as we walk inside. "It will be so nice to sleep in a real bed tonight."

Madden twists his torso back and forth to pop his back as we make our way to the elevator. "I think we're too old to sleep on couches."

I look up at him with a sad smile. "I'm glad we could be there with Sophie this week, though. She needed her family."

He pulls me into a hug as our elevator goes up. "I think you're right."

We get to our room and I take a quick shower, put on a baggy t-shirt, and throw my wet hair up into a messy bun. Madden takes his turn in the shower while I read a few chapters in my newest book. By the time he crawls into bed next to me, apprehension sets in. We haven't shared a bed since our debacle of an evening at the Wichita Fine Arts Society gala.

Before I can even take my glasses off, Madden grabs my novel, tosses it on the end of the bed, and pulls me into his broad, muscled chest. I laugh in surprise and he laughs with me, the sound oddly soothing. Neither of us has smiled or laughed in days.

"Now that we're alone, can we please talk about... us?" Madden asks.

I give him a faint smile and nod.

He leans back so he can see my face. "I deeply regret putting distance between us, Odette. I know that you've been keeping me at arms' length, and I understand why. I've given you some serious emotional whiplash." He pauses to collect his thoughts. "Honestly, I've given you no reason to trust me with the way I keep pushing you away, but... Odette, I don't want to push you away anymore. I'm not sure I could, even if I wanted to."

Madden rubs my back gently. "Please give me a chance to earn back your trust. That's all I want. And whatever challenges come our way, I promise to talk them out with you. No more hiding in the guest room."

I swallow the lump in my throat and take a deep breath. Watching Sophie grieve over the last few days made me feel so selfish for wasting precious time with Madden. I pushed him away to protect myself when I should've given him a second chance.

"Okay," I whisper. "I'll give you a chance. But please don't break my heart."

Madden

A day later, we're back in Wichita. I want to help Sophie settle in, but I've already been out of town for five days. I know that Paul is anxious to meet today and write my public apology.

Paul arrives at our apartment a little after 2:00 PM. I gesture for him to sit with Odette and I at the dining room table.

"How's your sister doing?" Paul asks first, his voice filled with sympathy.

"As well as can be expected," I say with a heavy sigh.

"Marie and I have been thinking about her."

"Thanks, Paul. I know Sophie would appreciate that."

Paul pulls his laptop out of his briefcase, then looks at me. "Oddly enough, your little hiatus may have worked to our advantage. The polls are more in your favor this week. Christopher is getting the brunt of negative attention now that the press knows he leaked the documents, and from his own place of employment, no less. The blowback has left a dent in Larry's previously pristine public image."

"Well, that's good news," Odette says with a smile.

Paul nods. "It is. However, the Democratic candidate has now pulled ahead of both you and Larry."

"Ah. That's not so good news." I frown, then shrug. "Well, no matter what, I still want to make a public apology. I'm done with the lies."

Odette puts her hand on top of mine. "No more hiding."

Paul cracks his knuckles. "Alright let's get to work. I think you should keep it short and sweet, though."

"You're the expert," I say with a smile.

Two hours later, my speech is written and the press conference is set for 10:00 AM the next morning.

Like Odette said: no more hiding.

Chapter 27

Odette

♥

M adden is quiet today, wiping his brow repeatedly as he drives to the courthouse for our press conference. He still holds my hand while he drives, though, absently rubbing his thumb along the back of my palm. I can tell that he's nervous. I am too. This public apology is much needed, but no one likes to air their regrettable decisions on national TV.

We pull up to the courthouse and Madden parks the car. We get out and check our reflections one more time in the car windows. He looks stately in his dark grey suit and navy blue tie, and I just hope I look presentable in my sage-green sheath dress and nude pumps. The outfits hardly matter, though; they're not what everyone will be talking about by the end of this.

A crowd of reporters and camera crews are gathered at the foot of the courthouse steps. As soon as they spot us walking from the parking lot, they all rush toward us, taking pictures and asking questions at once. David appears at my other side, putting some distance between me and the cameras.

Madden makes his way up the steps to the small podium Channel Ten News had set up. David takes my arm and guides me over to where my parents stand alongside Madden's down in the front row. I have a strange sense of deja vu when I remember the last time we were here for Madden's campaign announcement in January. But instead of Dr. and Mrs. Windell's eyes beaming with pride, they're now fraught with worry. Paul and Marie are here, too, standing near the steps a few feet from me.

I'm standing by my parents when, surprisingly, Kate appears from the crowd and sidles up beside me. She laces her arm through mine in solidarity and I can't help but tear up. It means so much to me that she's here. Though we haven't had a chance to talk about it yet, I'm sure that my lies hurt her, too.

Madden clears his throat to get everyone's attention. The crowd quiets down.

"My fellow Kansans, family, and friends," he begins, his voice ringing out strongly in spite of the nerves I know he's fighting. "What began as a strong desire to serve my country turned into lies and desperation to give myself the greatest chance of being elected. I recognize that my actions have given you cause to mistrust me and I deeply apologize for the hurt I've inflicted."

He pauses and looks down at his notes. Clearing his throat again, he suddenly slides his notes to the side. My eyes narrow. What is he doing?

"I had prepared an eloquent speech for today, but I don't want to wax poetic or fill your ears with meaningless words. The truth is, if I could go back in time, I'd marry Odette Hastings all over again."

My mouth gapes open as he looks into my eyes. I hear several gasps and murmurs from the crowd.

"I wouldn't marry her to help me get to Congress, though that was, admittedly, my original intention. No, if I could do it all over again, I'd marry her because I'm deeply, madly in love with her. She is an amazing, kind, and genuine person." He pauses and pulls our now-infamous marriage contract out of his suit pocket. Holding it up for everyone to see, he takes two corners and promptly rips it in half. Another murmur ripples through the crowd. "I should have torn up this stupid two-year contract months ago and convinced Odette to spend *all* of her days with me instead.

"I would love to be your Kansas state representative for the fourth district. It would undoubtedly be one of the greatest honors of my professional life and the fulfillment of a lifelong dream. My platforms are still the same and I'm still passionate about serving you. If you choose not to vote for me because of my deceit, I understand. I will pick myself up, dust myself off, and move forward with my life. But I can't do that without Odette.

"So, while I sincerely apologize for deceiving you, I will not apologize for marrying her. She is the best decision I've ever made."

My mouth is still gaping as Madden walks down the steps. The news crews, cameramen, and journalists clear a path for him, their cameras trained on him, as he walks toward me with purpose.

But he's not walking fast enough. I break from the crowd and walk the rest of the distance, meeting him in the middle of the lawn in front of the courthouse. We're surrounded by people, but I ignore them and focus on Madden. He takes my hands in his and gazes into my eyes. My heart feels like it's going to burst.

"I love you too, Madden. And I trust you with my heart." I get up on my tippy toes and bring my lips to his, only pulling back to smile so big that my face hurts. "I'm pretty sure I was smitten since the first time you wore those llama pajama pants."

"I thought you hated those?" He raises an eyebrow.

"Definitely didn't hate them." I wink.

He grins and pulls me in for another kiss. I hear clapping and whistling around us, pulling me back to reality.

With grins on our faces, we do our best to answer the barrage of questions from reporters, smiling as they snap photos. It's much easier to stand in front of them now that we're not pretending.

Over the last six weeks, Madden has continued campaigning and speaking at events. His heartfelt speech at the press conference clearly endeared him to some of his voters. In fact, our bizarre love story apparently sparked fascination among some of the public. To Kansas locals, we've pretty much turned into the American version of William and Kate.

We've kept close tabs on the polls. Miraculously, Madden has pulled ahead with a slim, five-point lead over Mark Jones. Meanwhile, Larry Highman is barely hanging on.

Sophie is all moved in with her parents now, and her room and the nursery are all set up. Madden's Mom and I even squeezed in a baby shower for her. It was a small gathering of just family and a few of Sophie's friends from high school. She cried during most of it, both out of joy and deep sadness. It has been difficult for her to experience all of this without Sam.

Tonight, she's coming over to our place for a movie night. I grabbed all of her favorites from the supermarket: pickles, sour patch kids, beef jerky, and frozen yogurt. Pregnancy is a strange thing.

I'm standing in the kitchen with my laptop on the counter—typing away—when I feel muscular arms slide around my waist. Madden's soft lips roam their way up my neck. Nothing makes me swoon more, and he knows it.

"Stop that! I'm finishing up a post for your Facebook page." I giggle and playfully swat his arm.

Madden tickles my sides. "Can't I flirt with my hot new social media manager?"

"When I told you that I missed working and wanted to freelance, I didn't realize that so much sexual harassment would be involved," I say with a sarcastic scowl.

He winks. "Whatever. You know you love it. Plus, you're doing an excellent job. I would've been a moron if I let someone else snatch up your amazing freelancing skills."

The doorbell rings and Madden goes to let Sophie in. She's 38 weeks pregnant, so he takes the snack tray with him. The man is surprisingly perceptive.

"Odette, get off that darn computer. It's movie time!" Sophie yells as she waddles through the door, grabbing a handful of Sour Patch Kids on her way past Madden.

"I know! I'm just finishing something up on Madden's website real quick," I say as I continue typing.

She smiles. "I hear his website has attracted a lot more traffic since you took over as social media manager."

With a flourishing click, I submit my post, then head into the living room to join them. "Where'd you hear that?"

She laughs. "I was eavesdropping during the campaign meeting at my parent's the other night. Did you know that my brother always refers to you as his campaign's *secret weapon*?"

"Does he really?"

"And I'm not even ashamed," Madden says with a grin.

Sophie sighs. "You guys are disgustingly adorable."

"Sorry, Soph." I give her a sympathetic look as I grab a few Sour Patch Kids and toss them in my mouth.

"It's okay. I love seeing you both so happy. And it works out that I get an awesome sister-in-law as a bonus."

I curl up between Sophie and Madden on the couch as we flip on a Netflix comedy. I notice that Sophie seems to grow quieter as the evening wears on, though. Somewhere in the middle of the movie, I glance over to make sure she's alright and find her looking incredibly uncomfortable.

I lean towards her and whisper, "Hey, you okay?"

She grimaces. "Yeah, I'm fine. I think the junk food gave me indigestion."

I get up and walk to the kitchen, thinking some water will probably make her feel better. When I return, her face is pale and her eyes are wide. She looks from me to Madden. "Um... I'm pretty sure my water just broke on your couch. Would either of you mind driving me to the hospital?"

"Holy cow! Of course." I plop my glass of water on the counter and grab my purse.

Madden jumps up, blurting something incomprehensible about hospitals and bags and babies. I hurry to him and place my hands on his shoulders. "Calm down and take a deep breath. You're not even the one giving birth."

Sophie doubles over with a laugh that quickly turns into a wheeze of pain. "Yup. Time to go."

⊸𝕖

Madden

The next day, Odette and I navigate through the large hospital to meet our niece. Despite coming to this hospital many times to see my dad in the surgical wing, I've never been to the Labor and Delivery floor. Luckily, it doesn't take us too long to find it, and we head straight to Sophie's room.

The room is dim and quiet as we enter, smelling faintly of antiseptic and baby powder. I hear the faint cry of another newborn a few doors down. My sister is resting in her hospital bed while my parents hover happily by the window, cooing over a tiny, pink burrito. I assume the baby is in there.

I stride over to take a peek and a wide grin spreads across my face. She's a precious little thing with a tuft of blonde hair, wispy little eyelashes brushing against her soft, pink cheeks, and perfect, tiny lips that resemble a cupid's bow. I look behind me to see Odette's reaction, but she's not there. After a quick glance around the room, I find her curled up in the hospital bed next to Sophie as she cries quietly.

I breathe in both the beauty and the heartbreak of the sight. Odette has this innate ability to sense the needs of others. It draws her to those who are hurting and in need of comfort, and she never hesitates to meet those needs. I remember when we visited the elementary school on Kansas Day, how she went straight to the shy kids and crouched beside them to offer encouragement. It's one of my many favorite things about her.

I join them cautiously, sitting on the edge of the bed near my sister. "It's gonna be okay, Soph. We're here for you."

She sniffles and wipes at her tears with the sleeve of her hospital gown, chin quivering. "I know, and I'm so grateful. But it's just not the same without Sam."

"You're right. And it's not fair, so just let it all out." Odette hands her some tissues.

I grab a tissue to dab at my now wet eyes. "Did you pick a name?"

Sophie looks up at me with a smile. "Samantha, in honor of her Daddy."

Odette brushes some hair from Sophie's face. "It's beautiful. I love it."

"Me too. Little Sam is the cutest baby I've ever seen." I grin.

Sophie laughs. "When is the last time you even saw a baby?"

I bring my hand to my chin. "Probably when Brooks was born. But she's definitely cuter than him."

Mom brings Samantha over to the bed. "Would you guys like to hold her?"

"I didn't think you'd ever give her over to anyone else." Dad comes up beside her with a laugh.

Mom just smirks and carefully hands the baby to Odette.

"Oh, Sophie, she's absolutely darling," Odette says as she kisses the top of Samantha's head.

Standing behind Odette, I look down at my niece. "I can't believe how tiny she is."

Sophie snorts. "She didn't feel so tiny a few hours ago."

I cover my ears. "Agh! I do not want to hear details."

Chapter 28

Odette

♥

Six months later.

T onight is *the* night, the one we've planned and waited for all year. Madden's campaign team has slaved away for days, setting up the conference center we rented out for the occasion. The room looks amazing. Red, white, and blue streamers streak above our heads, flag centerpieces anchor every table, and the buffet line even sports an ice sculpture of an American eagle—thanks to Madden's mom.

A general buzz of nerves and excitement permeates the room scattered about with people. Any moment now, we will receive word that Madden is the next congressional representative for the fourth district in the state of Kansas.

Or he will give his concession speech.

I have high hopes. Not only did Madden win the primaries in August, but he blew Larry Highman and Mark Jones away during their debate. Larry was so far behind Madden and Mark in the polls that he actually dropped out of the race after the debate. Tonight, though, we'll finally know the official results.

Needing to keep myself busy, I took some punch to my parents and made sure they're doing okay at their table. As I walk back toward

Madden, my eyes take him in with admiration. He's rocking a black suit with a red tie the same shade as my dress. He is as handsome as always. I savor any chance I get to see him in a suit; if tonight goes as planned, he'll be wearing suits pretty often in the future.

He spots me coming toward him and grins. "Get over here, wife."

"Of course, Mr. Congressman," I say in a sultry voice.

"Don't jinx it." He puts his arm around my waist. "By the way, this dress is driving me crazy, *Red*." He growls in my ear, and I giggle.

"Follow the sound of smooching and we are sure to find you two nearby." Paul smirks as he and Marie appear at our sides.

Marie chuckles. "Oh, now, not too long ago we were the same way!"

Paul kisses her cheek. "Very true."

Brooks and David join our little pow-wow. "Is it almost time? We didn't miss it, did we?" Brooks asks.

Madden takes a deep breath. "No, not yet. Any minute, though."

"I hope it's soon. I'm having trouble keeping Brooks away from the girls on the campaign team." David grumbles.

"I don't think they mind." Brooks winks.

We all roll our eyes in unison.

Suddenly, I hear a baby's cry and turn around to see Madden's parents coming up behind us with Sophie and little Sam. "Sorry, let me get her pacifier," Sophie says as she digs through her diaper bag.

"Oh, she's just excited. The cry was probably a cheer," I reply.

Surprise shoots through me when I notice that Madden's parents are holding hands. Maybe having a grandchild has helped them bond? I sneak a peek at Madden to see if he noticed as well. We make eye contact and both raise our eyebrows in question. It's like we have our own secret language, one of the unexpected perks of being married.

The entire room is filled with the drone of lighthearted conversation until Madden's phone rings. Everyone quiets down all at once.

No one so much as takes a breath as he answers.

"Hello, this is Madden Windell," he answers in his deep, confident voice. There's a pause as the person on the other end speaks.

Then a massive grin takes over Madden's face. "Wonderful! Thank you!"

He hangs up and we all anxiously await confirmation of what we already know. He pumps a fist in the air and shouts, "WE DID IT!"

The room erupts in triumphant chaos. Madden turns and sweeps me into a big hug, spinning me in circles as my feet fly off the ground. Red, white, and blue balloons rain down on us from the ceiling as the room cheers. When he finally releases me, he takes my hand and drags me up onto the stage with him. I laugh the whole way, reveling in his elation. I am profoundly proud of this man and so happy for him.

Madden steps up to the podium and takes a deep breath. "First, I have to thank everyone here in this room tonight. You were all a huge part of my success in this election." He pauses as the room erupts with more clapping and whistling. "Without all of you and my incredible wife, I never would've been able to become the first Libertarian congressman in Kansas! I hope to make you all proud in Washington and pave the way for change in this great state!"

The crowd roars in applause again. Madden pulls me into his side and we stand there smiling at each other, lost in this incredible moment as the room goes berserk around us.

Chapter 29

Madden

♥

I'm surprising Odette with a honeymoon eleven months late. We never had a free moment to take one, but I have the week of Thanksgiving off. In another month, I'll start spending a huge portion of my time in Washington D.C., so the timing couldn't be better.

Yesterday, I gave Kate the keys to the apartment to pack a suitcase for Odette. I hope she didn't go too crazy, since we'll only be gone for a week.

I wake up next to my wife in our apartment and gently stroke her back to wake her. "Good morning, Red. We need to get ready or we'll be late for our flight."

She drags one eye open and asks groggily, "What flight?"

"You didn't think I'd take you on a honeymoon?" I bring my hand to my chest in mock offense.

Her eyes fly open. "Wait, what is going on? Are we seriously flying somewhere?"

I point to the closet door. "If you look in the closet, you'll see your suitcase is already packed. You had better go get ready. We leave in an hour."

She flies out of bed and starts throwing her clothes on, stumbling into the bathroom to brush her teeth with only one pant leg on. "Where are we going?"

"I can't tell you. It's a secret."

"Not even a hint?" She calls out to me, though I can barely understand her through the muffled sound of gargling.

I tap on my chin. "Okay, one clue. We're flying to a different country."

She peeks her head around the bathroom doorway, her toothbrush hanging out of her mouth. "Tropical climate or cold?"

"I said *one* clue." I shake my head with a smirk, and she shoots me a playful glare.

Twelve hours later, we land in London. After grabbing our bags and picking up the rental car, I drive us to our next destination.

Halfway there, Odette's eyes fly wide open and she gasps, "Madden!"

I turn my head. Her eyebrows are about as high on her forehead as they can go. I'm instantly concerned. "What? Is everything okay?"

"Kate packed my suitcase?" She asks slowly.

I breathe again. "Of course."

She covers her face with her hands and groans.

"What? What could possibly be so bad about your best friend packing your suitcase?"

"You don't know Kate."

We arrive at our final destination after a few hours of driving: a beautiful, historic cottage nestled in the English countryside. The charming stone-walled cottage is surrounded by lush, green hills and is covered with a thick layer of English ivy. The windows and front door are rounded at the top giving the home a quaint look. It looks like Jane Austen herself could come walking out the door at any moment. It's even more ethereal than the photos online made it look. I park our rental car and we get out to stand in front of the picturesque home, taking in the pastoral paradise.

I slip my hand around my wife's waist and draw her against me. "I know it's not Pemberley, but I think it's the perfect spot for us to honeymoon."

Odette nuzzles into me. "I couldn't have imagined a better spot, not even in my dreams. Thank you for planning this."

Walking inside the lovely home, I set our suitcases by the door, and we begin to explore the place. Somehow, the whole cottage smells like lavender and freshly baked bread. The painted walls are pale yellow adorned with charming paintings of English landscapes, and there's a fireplace in the living room and the master bedroom upstairs. It's the perfect spot for a quiet honeymoon.

The house is a bit cold inside–as England isn't known for balmy weather in November–so I light the fireplaces while Odette takes her suitcase upstairs. She mentioned something about a bubble bath, probably unable to resist the antique clawfoot tub any longer.

Suddenly, I hear my wife scream from the top of the stairs. I drop everything and take the steps two at a time, bursting breathlessly into the bedroom, "What is it?!"

She motions toward her open suitcase. "This is what happens when you ask Kate to pack for me."

I look over and see the suitcase overflowing with delicate lace, feathers, and stilettos. I put it all together and burst out laughing. "Actually, it looks like she did an outstanding job. I'll definitely ask her to pack your suitcase every time we travel."

Her jaw drops. "Says the man who has a bag full of jeans and comfy sweaters!"

I put my arms around her and breathe huskily into her ear. "It'll be okay. I'll keep you warm."

"You better," she whispers as she leans toward me.

"Always." And then my lips claim hers

The End

Odette

♥

Epilogue

A month after our honeymoon, Madden had to make his first of many trips to D.C. He has only been gone for two weeks and I already miss him so much that my entire body feels achy and nauseous. Maybe it's just the January blues.

I'll get used to him traveling, eventually. I have to. I can't spend the next who knows how many years feeling sick like this.

Not wanting to spend another lonely night in our apartment, I'm on my way to Kate's house. We're having a much-needed girls' night. I've been looking forward to it all week. Sophie is coming, too, and I hope she brings little Sam so I can snuggle her.

Just thinking about snuggling that cute little baby is making me tear up. What has gotten into me?

I walk up the steps to Kate's house, walking carefully since they're slippery with snow. January in Kansas is dreary, cold, and honestly kind of miserable. I let myself into Kate's house, as usual, the smell of pizza hitting me instantly. I feel my stomach churn and bile rises in my throat. I put my hand to my mouth as a cold sweat breaks out on my skin.

Kate and Sophie look up from where they're sitting on the living room couch and rush toward me. They must've seen how green I look.

"Odette, are you alright? You look awfully pale." Sophie asks in concern.

I take a deep breath to make sure I won't puke. "Yeah, I think I'm fine now. I thought I was going to throw up."

Kate quirks an eyebrow and puts her hand on her hip. "Have you been feeling like this often lately?"

"Yes, actually. For the last week. I know this sounds ridiculous, but I think it's because I miss Madden." I shrug, and before I know it, tears are streaming down my face.

Sophie hands me a tissue, giggling. "Are you sure that's the *only* reason you might be feeling sick?"

I sniffle. "What do you mean?"

Kate puts her hand on my shoulder. "I think all the lingerie I packed for your honeymoon worked a little too well."

My jaw drops and I blink slowly, realizing what they're hinting at. "I hadn't even thought of that... but we've been so careful! We didn't want a baby right away."

"Accidents happen." Sophie smiles and jerks her head toward Samantha, gurgling contentedly in her car seat by the couch.

"I think I have a pregnancy test in the bathroom!" Kate exclaims and dashes down the hallway.

After digging around her diaper bag, Sophie hands me a peppermint. "This should help with the nausea."

Kate comes back down the hallway with a pink box in her hand. With a little running start, she slides in her fuzzy socks on the wood floors and skids to a stop in front of me. "I have one! It doesn't expire until next month!"

I take the box from her cautiously, eyeing their expectant expressions. "Surely you don't expect me to take it right this moment?"

"Odette Windell, if you don't get your little butt in the bathroom and take that test, I'm not letting you drink a single drop of wine tonight... And, obviously, if it's positive, I won't let you have any then either."

"Sounds like a lose-lose situation," I mutter, laying the sarcasm on thick. With a heavy sigh, I walk toward the bathroom to take the test, if only to prove to Kate and Sophie that I'm not pregnant.

The suggested three minutes pass by in excruciating slowness. After washing my hands, I close my eyes, take a deep breath, and brace myself as I look at the test results.

With the test in my hand, I shamble back out into the living room. When the girls see my shocked, pale face, they jump up and down with glee.

"I knew it! This is so exciting! Samantha will have a cousin!" Sophie practically bounces as little Sam coos happily in her carseat.

Kate wraps me in a hug. "I know this was a bit unexpected, but you're going to be such a great mom."

"I'm excited, really. I'm just... still processing." My vision blurs as my eyes become misty.

"Are you going to call Madden?" Sophie asks, then takes a bite of pizza.

I ponder a moment and shrug. "I hadn't thought that far ahead yet. He comes home in a few days, so I think I'd rather tell him in person. You guys can keep this a secret, right?" I give Kate a pointed look.

"We won't tell anyone!" Kate rolls her eyes. "I can't wait to hear about his reaction."

"Me either!" Sophie grins. "He's going to be an awesome dad. He was the best big brother growing up."

A rush of nerves prompts another wave of nausea. "He really is. I'm just not sure how he'll feel about a baby so soon."

⊰⊱

A few days later, I pick up Madden from the airport. As soon as his arms close around me at the arrival gate, I sigh and melt into him. We haven't been apart this long since we got married, so it feels wonderful to be in his arms again. Thankfully, the baby isn't upset by his cologne, which is a miracle, since he or she seems offended by every other scent the world offers.

We chat about the past few weeks he's been gone while we wait for his suitcase at the baggage claim and he holds my hand the entire time. It's nice to be missed. I know I'm probably grinning like a fool. Once he gets his luggage, we walk back to our car in the parking garage.

"I almost forgot how freezing cold Kansas is in January." He shivers as he puts his bags in the trunk.

"I know, it's been horrible. I get so cold at night. I miss my big, handsome space heater." I chuckle, and he wraps his arms around me again.

"Your heater is back, baby. I'll keep you warm just like I did in England." He winks, then opens my door for me.

I huff out a nervous laugh as I slide into the passenger seat.

We drive back to the apartment. I can tell from the way his hand keeps rubbing my leg that my husband only has one thing on his mind.

Boy, is he in for a surprise.

As soon as we walk inside the apartment, Madden rolls his suitcase in the door, throws his carry-on bag on the couch, and swoops me up in his arms, carting me off to the master bedroom.

He's about to toss me onto the bed when he suddenly and goes perfectly still. That's when I know he sees it: the tiny onesie laying on the bed that reads *Future Member of Congress.*

"Odette?"

"Yes, Madden?" I croon in an innocent voice.

He sets me gently back on my feet. "Does this mean what I think it means?"

"Well, speaking of keeping me warm in England..."

He slips his arms around my waist, looking a bit stunned. "Wow... obviously, this is unexpected.

"Are you okay?" I reach up to touch his face, concerned. I knew that this news might be hard for him.

"I feel surprisingly... excited." His eyes fill with tears.

I put my hands on both sides of his face and lean in to kiss him. He quickly plants a kiss on my lips before taking a step back and resting his large hand on my stomach.

I giggle. "There's not much of a baby bump yet."

"I can't wait to see you with a big belly."

"Well, come September, I'll be ginormous."

He slips his arms back around my waist. "Odette, you've made all my dreams come true... even the ones I didn't know I had."

♥

W ant to read more about Madden and Odette?
Click   here
(https://www.subscribepage.com/leahbrunnerwrites) to subscribe to
my newsletter and you'll receive a FREE bonus epilogue!

Trust me, you're going to want to read this.

❤️

☆☆☆☆☆

If you enjoyed this book, could you please do me a huge favor?

I would be incredibly grateful if you took a few moments to leave me a review.
Positive reviews on Amazon and Goodreads will help others find and read my book!
As an indie author, your support and feedback are vital! It also helps me give readers what they want in future books!
Many thanks in advance!

Acknowledgments

♥

This book wouldn't have been worth reading without the help of *many* wonderful people!

Thank you to Erin Packard Editing for muddling through those developmental edits with me. You helped me add so many necessary scenes, and the comment about America's Next Top Model became one of my favorite lines in the entire book! Your editing skills were invaluable.

Thank you to my lovely sister-in-law, Katie, and my best friend, Anna, for answering late-night phone calls and texts when I was struggling with plot issues–and for reading those very early, sloppy rough drafts. You both encouraged me so much and kept me going!

Thank you to the ladies on my BETA team, Amanda @my.bookish.heart, Reanne @faith.fiction.fact.fluff, and Meredith @bookandacupofcocoa! You ladies were amazing and your input and helpful comments played a huge role in making this novel readable.

Lastly, thank you to my ARC team! It made my heart so happy that you were excited to read this book. Thank you for all your support!

About The Author

♥

Leah Brunner is a Kansas girl at heart, but currently resides in Northern California with her husband and three children.

They're an Air Force family and have had the pleasure of living all over the United States. Leah spends most of her time writing, reading, and petting her Maine Coon cat.

As a child, Leah had a vivid imagination and dreamt of becoming an author someday. After reading hundreds of books during the 2020 pandemic, she finally took the plunge and wrote her first novel, *A Love Unexpected.*

To stay in the loop and hear about upcoming releases, visit Leah's website and subscribe to her newsletter! https://app.mailerlite.com/sites/preview/4127233

CPSIA information can be obtained
at www.ICGtesting.com
Printed in the USA
LVHW112023260422
717291LV00004B/244

9 781737 015604